I0817946

# CAUGHT YOU

(A Rylie Wolf FBI Suspense Thriller —Book 2)

Molly Black

**Molly Black**

Debut author Molly Black is author of the MAYA GRAY FBI suspense thriller series, comprising six books (and counting); the RYLIE WOLF FBI suspense thriller series, comprising three books (and counting); and the TAYLOR SAGE FBI suspense thriller series, comprising three books (and counting).

An avid reader and lifelong fan of the mystery and thriller genres, Molly loves to hear from you, so please feel free to visit www.mollyblackauthor.com to learn more and stay in touch.


ISBN: 978-1-0943-9398-8

**BOOKS BY MOLLY BLACK**

**MAYA GRAY MYSTERY SERIES**
GIRL ONE: MURDER (Book #1)
GIRL TWO: TAKEN (Book #2)
GIRL THREE: TRAPPED (Book #3)
GIRL FOUR: LURED (Book #4)
GIRL FIVE: BOUND (Book #5)
GIRL SIX: FORSAKEN (Book #6)

**RYLIE WOLF FBI SUSPENSE THRILLER**
FOUND YOU (Book #1)
CAUGHT YOU (Book #2)
SEE YOU (Book #3)

**TAYLOR SAGE FBI SUSPENSE THRILLER**
DON'T LOOK (Book #1)
DON'T BREATHE (Book #2)
DON'T RUN (Book #3)

# CHAPTER ONE

Lila Garrity left the Bozeman Trail Steakhouse in Buffalo, Wyoming, at a little after closing time, headed for Interstate 86, the Highway Thru Hell.

It had been a long night, waiting tables, all for less than thirty bucks in tips. Her ego hurt just as much as her feet. Forcing those thoughts away, she pulled out of the parking lot onto the mostly empty streets of downtown Buffalo. She had to get to her place in Sheridan, about sixty miles down Interstate 86. Her husband and her puppies were waiting for her.

Of course, Bronco and Cowboy weren't really puppies anymore. They were full-grown Great Danes, almost as big as she was. That wasn't saying much, since Lisa was petite in every way; but for a dog, that was some feat. And her boys wanted to go hiking in the Bighorn Mountains tomorrow morning. She'd always been a pushover where they were concerned.

As she drove her old Chevy Silverado past the closed-down Hardee's and the Quik-Mart gas station, her phone began to ring. It was her husband of five years, Sheridan's best mechanic, Ace Garrity.

"Hey, Ace," she said when she picked up. "I'm out of that hellhole. Finally."

"Well, it's about time. It's almost midnight. Those Yankees treat you well?"

She sighed and glanced over at the cup holder, where she'd stashed the night's tips. A bunch of big-time New Yorkers had come in for a weekend of roughing it, part of a bachelor party. Ace had joked that "roughing it," to them, meant not having a Starbucks on every corner. That was okay—they'd infuse her home state with some tourism cash, and that was never a bad thing. But instead of giving her the big-city tips she'd expected, they'd treated it like a regular bachelor party, getting drunk and groping her and trying to stuff a couple meager dollar bills down her shirt. "I wish."

"Aw come on, you're teasin'. How can they resist a sweet thing like you?"

"Oh, believe me. They're too stuck up for the likes of me. They throw around their money on hundred-dollar scotches, and tip me hardly nothin'. I need to get home and get a shower to get their big-city grease off me."

"It's waiting for you, baby," he said, and she could hear the smile in his voice. "I'll have a nice Rattlesnake waiting for you, too. You be careful now, girl. Drive safe."

"I will."

She could practically taste the whiskey of that Wyoming Rattlesnake as she disconnected the call, just as she was driving up the ramp onto 86. She shuddered as she put her foot to the gas pedal. Though she'd been driving this route for three years, ever since she got the job waiting tables at Bozeman, it never seemed to get any easier. Especially knowing the reputation this highway had among locals.

Its name, the Highway Thru Hell, was apparently very well deserved.

Normally, Lila would've laughed. She always did, whenever people talked about creepy stuff like ghosts and urban legends. She never hid her eyes during horror movies or got the willies when she was home alone at night. And the moniker sounded overly dramatic.

But for this highway? It fit. There was something about it. There had been hundreds of unsolved murders along this stretch of road, ever since it opened in 1978. Sure, it was a big stretch, since Interstate 86 went from Seattle to Eau Claire, but these parts were some of the least populated in the whole country. Even one murder in this corner of Wyoming was too many. And there had been several. A few weeks ago, it was the case of that crazy man who was stringing people up like human sacrifices, on mile posts. He'd been caught, yes, which should've helped her breathe easier.

But it *hadn't* gotten easier. The highway was never busy, especially at this time of night. The few trees that surrounded it were leafless, skeletal, like sentries, warning her to stay out. And a strange, thick haze, the kind that hovered over a cemetery in the dead of night, always seemed to hug the road, making it eerie as hell. Not to mention the full moon, hanging silent in the sky half-obscured by sinister clouds.

As she accelerated up the ramp, onto the long, flat, two-laned road, she felt like the only traveler there. Not another set of headlights to be seen.

Another shudder. She reached over and turned on the radio. Kenny Chesney sang "There Goes My Life." She sang along with the words, trying to calm herself down, wondering, not for the first time, why she had to work at Bozeman. There was another steakhouse, right in Sheridan, and they'd had a Help Wanted sign in the window. Five-hundred dollar signing bonus, too, if she stayed on a full year. It'd be a five-minute commute from their trailer. She was tempted by it, every time she drove past.

It was Ace who'd mentioned it, a couple weeks ago. Back then, she'd argued. "The manager at Bozeman loves me. And he's such a sweetheart. Plus, I have seniority there. I get to pick my shifts," she'd told him, slapping his beefy shoulder.

Usually, she picked the lunch rush. But when she'd heard a big bachelor party was coming in for dinner, she'd picked this stupid night shift, hoping those high-and-mighty Yankees would give her big tips. She'd been wrong.

The Big Wyoming Steakhouse in Sheridan was looking better and better, with every passing day.

*I should just check it out. Maybe tomorrow, after Big Horn with the puppies, I'll stop in and get an application. Can't hurt to just try.*

Decision made, she turned up the radio and started to groove to an oldie but goodie from Alan Jackson: "Don't Rock the Jukebox."

That was when she noticed the headlights in her rearview mirror. They were miles back, though, so far away that the headlights bled together into one tiny pinpoint of light instead of two.

It wasn't alarming. This was the interstate. Of course, there would be other cars on the road. Not many, but some. She ignored it, fastening her eyes on the road and singing louder.

But the next time she glanced in the mirror, the lights were much closer. Probably only a half-mile or so back.

*Geez, he's really racing. Or am I going too slow?*

She lowered her eyes to her speed gauge. The speed limit here was 80, and she was going 90. She couldn't push that old Chevy truck, a relic from her daddy, any faster than that, or its transmission would probably bottom out.

But this crazy guy had to have been going at least 100. Maybe 110, with the way he was gaining on her.

She wrapped her hands tightly around the steering wheel and forced herself to breathe normally. She was in the slow lane. She'd simply do what her daddy always told her to do: *Move to the side and let the crazies wrap themselves around a tree, if they want. No skin off your nose.*

But then the lights filled her rearview mirror, blinding her.

He was right on her tail. So close, she found herself bracing for impact.

"What the hell?" she grouched, rolling down her window and sticking her hand out, motioning for him to pass. "Pass me, dude. You want an invitation?"

That had no effect. The truck—she could see it was a pick-up, now, but a big one, since its headlights were shining straight into her back window—shimmied back and forth violently in the lane, but refused to pass.

She let out a huff of breath. It was probably one of those damn Yanks. There were all kinds of city people, moving out here for the wide-open spaces, thinking they owned the road. Not a one of them knew how to drive.

"Personal space! What are you, afraid to get in the fast lane? Jerk!" she muttered to herself, shaking her head. "What the hell does he want from me?"

She did just as her father had taught her. She eased off the gas and slowed a little, still motioning for him to go around her.

When that didn't work, she checked the mileposts. She was at least two miles from the next exit. Maybe if she could get there, she could pull off, and he'd go on ahead and leave her alone.

Lila blinked, squinting in the bright light reflecting off her mirror, trying to see a hint of the man behind the wheel. All she could see were two thick hands, with knob-like knuckles, clutching the steering wheel. Beyond that, a large form in shadow. It could've been anyone.

She dropped her speed even more, hoping the guy would finally get the hint.

He did. He veered sharply to her left, and she let out a sigh of relief as he moved up around her bumper.

This was where Ace would've given the guy the finger.

But she knew better. Lila had read about far too many road rage cases in the news, and she didn't want to be one of those statistics. She wanted this to end. Now.

*All right, all right. Just stare straight ahead as he passes. And then he can drive as fast as he wants, away from you.*

She clutched the steering wheel and did just that, staring at the long, dark road ahead as the truck pulled up beside her, into the passing lane. She tried to get into the beat of the music, but she couldn't help but notice the features of the truck. It was a gray one, and fairly nice.

*A shame that its idiot owner will probably wreck it with his reckless driving.*

For some reason, though, he seemed to have trouble passing her. She slowed even more, glancing down at the speedometer. She was only going sixty, now.

And so was he.

Now, they were practically drag-racing, lined up together. She sped up. He matched her. She slowed down. He matched that, too.

"What the . . .?" she murmured, gnawing on her lip.

She was vaguely aware that the dark tinted, passenger-side window of the truck was powering down. Begging to be looked at.

*No you don't,* a voice inside her said. But she couldn't help it.

Reluctantly, her eyes swept left, and a strange thing happened. She immediately wished she hadn't looked, and yet, she couldn't *stop* looking.

There, in the darkened cabin of the truck, was a horrific face with a leering, psychotic grin, eyes wild. At first, she thought it was a Halloween mask, that the man was trying to scare her. But the eyes were too real. Eyes that said, *You're mine.*

A cold frisson of fear jolted its way down her spine. A single thought planted itself in her head. *Must get away.*

She stamped on the gas.

Before she could get past him, though, she saw him suddenly throw his steering wheel to the right.

There was a sickening crunch of metal, and suddenly, her car went fishtailing. She tried to correct, to stamp on the brakes, but that only made things worse. At this speed, she quickly found herself losing control, the truck misbehaving underneath her, going in ways she hadn't intended. She found herself careening straight for the shoulder. She tried to correct again, fishtailing more, stomping on the brakes and trying to swerve back on the road, but it all happened so fast. The wheel was spinning beneath her hands, uncontrolled, and the tires underneath her squealed like a stuck pig. Everything else was a blur around her.

When she regained focus, she lost gravity. She found herself airborne. Her head scraped the cab's ceiling and the seatbelt sliced into her shoulder as she saw, with widening eyes, the gully beneath her, illuminated by the headlights.

Gripping the wheel tight, she closed her eyes and braced herself.

The impact was breathtaking, making every inch of her body reverberate with the shock of it. The windshield shattered, sending shards of sharp glass spraying against her skin. The sucking sound of the airbag deploying rang in her ears as in a white wave; it pushed her back against the headrest. She tasted something chalky and earthy, mixed with the metallic tang of blood.

The truck juddered to a stop, she heard the ding, ding, ding of something on the dashboard. Probably the damn Check Engine light, which was always on.

She found herself hanging over the airbag, gravity pulling her down to it, but the seatbelt keeping her in place.

She groped in the cup holder for her phone, but all she found there were a few dollar bills. Her phone was gone.

She tried to shove away the airbag. The cabin was dark, save for the light of a single headlight that seemed to reflect back at her. Her vision and brain were hazy, Half-formed thoughts idling through it—*I've been in an accident. I need help.*

She reached down, toward the ground, feeling along the carpeting for her cell. When she couldn't reach, she felt the way down the canvas strap, struggling to find the button for the seatbelt release, at her hip. When she depressed it, her body gave way, falling upon the sagging airbag, drooping toward the dashboard. It allowed her a few more inches, so that her fingertips were able to scrape the carpet in search of her phone.

She wasn't thinking, at that moment, about the man with the leering grin who'd run her off the road.

Well, she *had* been thinking that a jerk like that wouldn't call 9-1-1, so he wasn't worth thinking about. Damn hit-and-run driver.

She certainly didn't expect him to have pulled over to the side of the road after the collision, not far from where she'd careened off the highway.

So when the door was ripped open, she'd expected someone else. A passing traveler, maybe, ready to jump into action and help her to safety.

She didn't expect the person to reach in, tangle his hand in her long hair, and tear her from her seat. Barely conscious, she felt herself being dragged into the cool air of night, then thrown unceremoniously on the hard ground.

"What . . .?" she managed, her vision swimming. She saw the dark sky. She felt the hard ground. She ached. All over, she ached.

She tried to roll over into a fetal position, but then he grabbed her by the hair again, tearing strands from her scalp. She yelped as he yanked her away. Up. Up the embankment, toward the highway.

Lila saw the tires of the pick-up in her tilted vision. Coming closer, closer. The pain turned to numbness. Everything in her body felt swollen, especially her tongue and her head. She couldn't bring herself to scream, or to even think of words to say.

He brought her around to the back of the truck. It was a relief when he let go of her hair. She rolled over on the hard surface and stared up at the starry sky.

Then he pulled something over her, closing her in. Locking it.

*A tonneau cover. Ace always wanted one of those for his pick-up.*

Then the truck started up, and the engine roared underneath her. She felt the gravel on the side of the road, pinging against the truck's tires, and closed her eyes.

She let the rhythm of the truck's engine carry her away.

# CHAPTER TWO

Rylie Wolf sat in the conference room of the FBI field office in South Dakota, the contents of a cold case file of a murdered hitchhiker spread out before her. Her mind swam with possibilities as she stared into space, without seeing.

"Think fast," someone in the conference room said. Or at least, she thought. She wasn't paying attention. She was too busy, trying to put together the pieces of this case that had been plaguing them for the past week, ever since she'd come back to work after solving the case of the serial killer who'd strung his victims up on mileposts along highway 86.

"Shit," the voice grumbled suddenly, stirring her from her thoughts.

Her partner, Michael Brisbane, was frantically grabbing fast-food napkins from the center of the table, trying to corral the creeping spill of a busted OJ container. It rested on its side, sadly defeated, a few inches away from her case file.

She jumped to action, yanking her papers away from the spill. "What are you—" She groaned, "Nice job, Brisbane! What were you trying to do?"

He threw a mountain of napkins on the biggest part of the spill and sighed. "I thought I was trying to be nice and give my partner an OJ. But I didn't realize she was on another planet. Sorry for being nice."

"Oh." Rylie smiled as he tossed the sopping napkins into the trash. "Thanks, anyway. I was just thinking."

"Clearly," he said with a laugh, grabbing the other OJ from his pocket and pushing it over to her. "Here. Have mine."

"Oh, no. I'm not thirsty. But thanks."

"I'll take it!" Beeker, the FBI's IT guy, said from the corner, his nose still buried in his computer. The kid was in his early twenties, and had probably been recruited to join their ranks right out of high school. He didn't know much about hygiene or professionalism, which was apparent from his long chin-whiskers and rumpled STAR WARS t-shirt and jeans.

"You have legs. Get yourself to the vending machine and get one yourself," he said to Beeker, as he opened it, tossing back a swig. Then he motioned with his chin. "What case is that? Is that about the tip Clive McDougal gave us?"

"Yep. Chrissy Johnson," she explained, pushing it across to him.

"Clive. What a scumbag," he mumbled, shaking his head as he read the file. "So what about it?"

Her partner wasn't one to toss around derogatory epithets lightly, but in this case, that one was well-deserved. Clive *was* a first-rate scumbag. While hunting down that serial killer, they'd stumbled across the case of a man who'd kidnapped a young girl, but luckily, Rylie and Michael Brisbane had rescued her before it was too late. But he'd been facing life in prison, and so he gave them a variety of tips in an effort to get a reduced sentence. One of them was the name of another trucker who he thought was involved in the disappearance of other hitchhikers: most recently fifteen-year-old Chrissy Johnson, in Montana.

The guy's name was Vin. He drove for Swiftline Express, out of Missoula. Rylie and Michael had done a bunch of investigating and calling and had found a few possibilities. The most promising one was Gary Vinton. According to the trucking company's logs, he'd been in the general area during a couple of the murders.

But then he'd dropped off the edge of the earth.

From their research, they'd learned he collected his last paycheck and never showed up for work again, abandoned his last known address, and just disappeared, without a word to anyone. No one—his wife, his family members, his friends--had seen him in months.

So no Gary Vinton. She paged through the file on him, turning to the most recent photograph, taken a few years ago. It showed a thirty-something year old guy with a fairly long, scraggly beard, and a muscle shirt baring thick, tattooed biceps. His arm was around a pretty blonde in short shorts and cowboy boots. They were standing in front of his rig, which they'd learned happened to be rented from Swiftline Express.

The next thing she knew, her partner was snapping his fingers in her face.

She blinked. "What?"

He pointed out the door. "You got a call. Out there. Didn't you hear?"

She stood. No, when she got involved in a case, everything seemed to disappear. She hated to leave the file alone, even for a second, so she jogged out to the front desk, where the receptionist was waiting. "Line five," she said, motioning to a nearby phone.

Rylie picked up and depressed the button. "Hello?"

"There's my baby girl."

"Hal?"

"That's right," he said in that slow, easy way of his. "You haven't called me in a while. Got the feeling that maybe you forgot about me."

She smiled. "Never! How could I?" He could always bring a smile to her face, even during her worst days. "Why didn't you call me on my cell?"

"I did. You never pick up."

She laughed. "And it's far too much to ask you to leave a message, huh? Or text?"

"What's that?" he said, in a way that made her unsure if he was joking. He was over sixty, and probably the most old-school, stuck-in-his-ways person she knew. "I thought you were going to stop in and pay me a visit while you were still in Wyoming?"

She winced. She had promised that, but the idea of going back to her old home made her stomach pool with dread. She'd grown up on the property right next to Hal Buxton's ranch. He was a down-to-earth, good guy, more of a father to her than her own dad had been. She'd been meaning to visit Hal, the big, burly old cowboy, but didn't want to dredge up old memories. Plus, if she did that, she'd probably have to visit her dad, too.

So yes. She'd been avoiding his calls. Every time his number popped up on her phone, she let it go straight to voicemail. "Yeah . . . sorry about that."

"I get it, I get it. This ain't your home, now."

It had been, once upon a time, when she was young. She and her older sister Maren and her mother and father had lived happily on that tract of land outside of Cody, Wyoming. But their peace had been shattered one day, at a remote campground. Her mother and friends had been murdered in cold blood, and Maren had simply vanished. After that, her father had completely retreated into himself.

But Rylie didn't really have a home, anymore. She'd moved to Seattle in effort to escape those old memories, but they never went away.

Now, here she was, solving crimes out of the Rapid City, South Dakota, field office of the FBI, not far from where her life had been completely destroyed. "I don't really have a home, anymore, Hal."

"Yeah, well. People say home is where family is. You speak to your dad lately?"

"No. Not in years, Hal. Not since I moved out to Seattle. We don't have much to say to each other. You know that. He doesn't even know I'm back here," she said, as curiosity got the best of her. "Why? Have you?"

"Nah. You know Rick Wolf don't like me. Besides, he stays to himself. Whenever I go into town, I never see him."

She cringed, wondering if he was all right. Part of her hated that she still cared about him, since he'd stopped caring about everything, including her, after the horrors of that day. He'd taken to drinking and barely got out of bed. He let his property go to hell, skipped a bunch of payments, and lost it to foreclosure. Now, he lived in the town of Cody, in some broken-down apartments behind the Wal-Mart. Rylie had only heard that in passing—she hadn't seen him in ages.

But he was still her father. And in a way, she understood. Her life had gone to hell, just as his had. She didn't think she'd ever get past the memory of her mother and Rose and her best friend, Kiki, lying in a growing puddle of blood outside their family RV.

The memory danced through her mind again, and as usual, she cringed. "Geez, Hal. He could be dead for a year in his apartment, and no one would be the wiser."

"Nah. Cody's a small place. People have seen him around, or so I hear through the grapevine. I just haven't. And that red beater of his keeps moving around the parking lot outside his place. He's all right. But you know your daddy."

Yeah, she did. She might not have seen him in years, but he was one leopard who'd never change his spots. He kept away from people. Especially her.

In that way, they were alike. Even just seeing each other stirred up too many unpleasant memories. Better to let them lie.

"Hal? If you do see him, do me a favor and don't tell him you spoke to me. If he wants to get in touch, he has my number. I haven't changed my cell phone in years."

"Right . . . even though you never pick up."

"I've been busy!"

"Sure," he said, in a way that made her think he didn't believe a word she said.

Hal had always been intuitive, that way. He could read her like a book, even a state away. "I'm sorry, Hal. Maybe soon? I'll give you a call when I'm in the neighborhood."

*Which is probably never.*

He was probably thinking that, too, but at least, he didn't press her on it. "Sure, baby girl. Talk to you soon."

As she hung up, she glanced over to the conference room and saw Michael Brisbane waving frantically. Some men were blandly handsome, vanilla, with pleasant features that were hardly memorable. But every feature on Michael's face stood out, from his chiseled jaw to his piercing blue eyes. Yet they all worked together in perfect harmony, as if none of them wanted to take center stage. Right now, his sculpted cheekbones were tinged red. It looked like he'd been trying to get her attention for a long time, but of course, she'd been practicing her tunnel vision and completely tuned him out. "What?" she asked, approaching him.

He held up a sheet of paper, a triumphant look on his face. "Just got a tip from the state police in Buffalo. Found a hitchhiker who said she met a guy named Gary Vinton, in a red Toyota Tacoma, on our favorite highway, while she was trying to catch a ride. Said the guy was acting really weird and so she thought she'd report it."

Her eyes widened. "Really?" She rushed to grab her purse and cell phone. "All right. Let's get over there. Quick!"

# CHAPTER THREE

As Rylie drove, she shot annoyed glances at Michael Brisbane, who sat in the passenger seat, eating pistachio nuts and powering down the window every so often to spit out the shell.

Not only that, but they were red pistachios, and his fingers were the color of cherries.

He may have been pretty, but her partner was pretty gross. Not only that, but he had a habit of talking. All the time. About absolutely nothing. The man could talk to a mountain and get it to talk back.

He handed her the paper bag, full of them, chewing noisily. "Want some? My momma always said that pistachios are pretty darn good for you. Nuts, you know. They got protein, and antioxidants, and--"

"No, and please stop talking like Forrest Gump," she mumbled, screwing up her face in disgust as he went to spit out another shell and missed. The shell—and his spit—landed on the window ledge of the door. "And let me ask you a question. Do you actually work at that?"

He flicked it out and grabbed another shell. "At what?"

She pointed at the bag. "That. Being gross. It sounds like feeding time at the monkey house."

"Aw, come on. I'm starving."

"You are always hungry, Brisbane. I doubt you even know what an antioxidant does. You probably just heard that buzzword on a commercial. Like, *it's got electrolytes,* so it's got to be good for you."

"Actually, antioxidants fight free radicals in your body, which might help prevent cancer, and—"

"What's a free radical?"

He paused. "Uh . . .well . . ."

"See, you don't know."

"No, I do. It's a radical that's not incarcerated." He grinned, satisfied, and popped another nut into his mouth.

"Right. Do you always have to eat in my truck, too?" she asked him as they crossed the border into Wyoming. "Can't you just . . . I don't know . . . control your stomach?"

"This is a long ride, Wolf," he said, stretching his arms over his head and yawning. "It's not my fault you never want to eat anything. It's a wonder you don't waste away."

"All right. Just don't mess up the upholstery with those red fingers of yours."

"Yes, sir." He saluted her, grinning.

That was Brisbane. One would think that FBI agents would be a lot more morose. They saw the worst of the worst, in criminals. Rylie had seen her share, all her life, even before the FBI, and so she'd become appropriately jaded. Brisbane, though? He acted like every day was a trip to Disney World. The guy didn't seem to have a "sad" switch. Or an "angry" one, either. In fact, he was so positive, she rarely saw him without a smile on his movie-star gorgeous face.

*I guess when you look that good, you don't have very much to be sad about,* she thought.

But he had to have seen his share of bad cases. He'd been part of his field office's BAU, too, just like she had been. And he wasn't new to the agency. Somehow, though, he managed to stay happy and light, and joke even during the worst of situations.

And he had an appetite . . . All. The. Time. Even after they'd seen some of the grisliest crimes, ones that would make Rylie not want to eat for days, all he could think about was food.

Rylie just didn't understand it. Part of her was disgusted by it, part amused . . . but mostly, she felt jealous about it. *If only I could be that oblivious and not let everything hit me so hard.*

But she couldn't. Maren, her missing sister, always came to her mind. Every day, Rylie thought of Maren. She wondered if she was still alive. She wondered what had happened that day. But most of all, she desperately wanted to bring the criminals responsible for ripping apart her family to justice.

It was the reason she'd become an FBI agent, too. The reason she was known for taking chances. The reason she did everything possible to get her man.

She imagined every criminal as responsible for Maren's kidnapping and her mother's death . . . and she simply *had* to put every ounce of herself into it.

She owed it to them.

Suddenly, Brisbane was snapping his fingers in her face again. Red ones, this time. "What?"

"You zoned again. I was telling you it's this next exit."

She blinked at the sight of exit 80, quickly coming up. "Wait, I thought you said it was a hitchhiker on the road? *This* road?"

"Yeah. But she's not on the road now. It happened hours ago. The police took her to the station to get her statement."

"Oh," she said, disappointed. Maybe this guy was Gary Vinton, but if it'd happened hours ago, it meant he was probably long gone.

She veered to the right and followed the signs to the police station. A moment later, they pulled into the near-empty parking lot. She gathered up her bag and phone and they went inside.

In the waiting room, a police officer was sitting with a young girl who couldn't have been more than eighteen. She had auburn curls that went down her back and matching freckles on her cheeks and pale legs under a denim skirt, and her hands were stuffed into the pockets of a gray hoodie. She bounced her foot nervously on the ground as she spoke to the officer who was sitting with her.

"Officer Preston?" Brisbane asked, showing his credentials. "We spoke on the phone. I'm Michael Brisbane of the FBI, and this is R—"

"Rylie Wolf," she said, nodding at him as she pulled out her own ID. She couldn't help it; she always like to take control of any interview she was part of. "Is this the hitchhiker?"

The officer nodded. "This is Nina Maxwell. Her car broke down around milepost 65. We had it towed to a body shop across the street, and she's called some family to come and get her in the meantime."

"Thank you, Officer."

Nina's hand was like ice as Rylie shook it. Her eyes were full of worry. She said, in a low voice, "I know, hitchhiking's illegal. But I was desperate. You gotta—"

"That's not what we're questioning you about," Rylie assured her, sitting beside her. "We're more interested in the man who stopped to pick you up. Can you tell us a little more about what happened? Start from the beginning."

She nodded, shivering. "Well, I was going to my boyfriend's place in Sunshine, because he was going to be in a rodeo, his first time. We met during a high school camp in Lander. Anyway, my car just started going haywire on me. All these lights lit up the dashboard like the Fourth of July and I lost power. I called my boyfriend, Seth, and he said it was probably the catalytic converter, and that I should call Triple A. So I tried, but my phone ran out of charge." She sighed. "So when this guy showed up in a pick-up, I thought it was the answer to my prayers.

He didn't have a phone, but he offered to drive me to the next exit so I could make a call."

"Did this man say his name?"

She nodded. "Gary. He was pretty young. Maybe like thirty? He had a blonde moustache and he was kind of cute, too. So at first I didn't mind it too much when he started flirting with me. I thought he was being nice. But then he got really creepy, really fast."

That fit the description of Gary based on the photo in his file. Rylie exchanged a glance with Michael, whose eyebrows narrowed. "Creepy, in what way?"

"Well, he was telling me I had nice legs, and then he told me he always wanted a girl with freckles. And he kept looking me up and down and, licking his lips. Just making me feel really skeeved out. Then . . . he went and missed the exit!"

"He did?"

She nodded. "Yeah. He said the nearest exit didn't have any place to stop, but that he was sure he could find a pay phone at the next exit."

"And what did you do then?" Rylie asked, pulling out her notepad and writing, *Gary, blonde, moustache, 30.*

"I told him to let me off!" she said with conviction, as if it was obvious. "I told him I'd find a ride with someone else."

"And did he let you off?" Brisbane asked.

She shook her head. "Not at first. He reached over and tried to grab me. But Seth—my boyfriend-- had showed me a couple of moves. I bit his arm, right here." She pointed to the fleshy part of his forearm. "He screamed, called me a bitch, and pulled to the side of the road. Practically pushed me out. Then he tore off, like a bat out of hell. And that was it."

"What kind of car was he driving?" Rylie asked.

"It was a black truck. I'm not good with trucks, but I think it was one of the bigger ones. A heavy duty, work truck, you know? Windows all dark."

Rylie nodded and wrote that down and Michael said, "You know anything else about him? Did he say where he was heading? Where he was from?"

She thought for a moment. "Well, I told him I was heading to a rodeo and he said he liked those, and he'd once been in the Cheyenne Frontier Days, years ago, when he was a kid. I got the feeling from the things he was pointing out that he lived around here. Like the different exits. And he knew all about my hometown. But he was mostly asking me questions about myself."

Rylie wrote down *Likely Wyoming native- Cheyenne?*

Then she looked up at the officer. "Have you put out an APB on this guy? Blonde, moustache, thirty, black truck?"

The officer shook his head. "No . . . not yet."

Rylie rolled her eyes. "What are you waiting for? Get on it."

"*Please*," Brisbane added, giving her his *be nice* look, which he seemed to give her every hour of the day.

"*Please*," she parroted, grimacing at him.

The officer nodded and headed off behind the front desk.

"Thank you, Miss Maxwell," Brisbane said, touching her forearm lightly. "I'm sure this must've been a harrowing incident for you. Are you going to be all right?"

She looked up at him, grateful and clearly a little starstruck, by the way she leaned into his touch. Rylie hadn't been his partner long, but she'd already noticed that he had an effect on women. A big one. "Oh. Yes, thank you," the girl gushed, batting her eyelashes. "You're very nice."

Rylie glared at him. "Agent? Can I talk to you alone for a moment?"

He looked up, smiled at the girl, and said, "Sure thing."

She pulled him to the side and said, "This guy in this black truck could definitely be Chrissy Johnson's kidnapper. If it happened a few hours ago, there's a chance he's still in the area."

Brisbane nodded. "Yeah. We should sit tight here, put out an APB, and see if anyone from the state police has seen him on the road."

Rylie shook her head. She never liked to sit tight, ever. "Have we compiled all the other cases that he might be responsible for? If we do bring him in for questioning, I want to make sure we have all of that information available so that we can catch him in a lie."

"We do. You know we do."

Yes, she knew that. They had the files in her truck, and she'd practically memorized them by now. They'd been pouring over case files, and come up with half a dozen kidnappings and murders of hitchhikers in Wyoming and Montana, most of them along Interstate 86, over the last five years. All of them, like Chrissy Johnson and Nina Maxwell, had been girls younger than twenty-two, pretty, Caucasian. Only two had been found, dead, their bodies so badly decomposed it was difficult to reconstruct what had happened to them.

"I do. I just don't want to leave anything up to chance," she said with a sigh.

He gave her an encouraging smile. "We're not. Trust me. We're going to get this son of a bitch this time. I can feel it."

Even if he was a messy eater, his positivity did help temper her normal doom-and-gloom outlook. This time, she appreciated it. "I hope so."

"I know so!" he said, pumping his fist. "But give me your keys. I'll go out and get those files from your truck so we can put together a game plan. All right?"

She reached into her pocket and handed them to him. "Thanks."

Just then, the officer came into the waiting room and cleared his throat. "Agents. We just got a call about a crash, about a mile down the interstate."

"A crash?" Rylie shook her head. "Sorry."

Brisbane clarified, "That's a job for your men. We don't deal in motor vehicle accidents."

The kid nodded, but hesitated.

"Is there something else?" Rylie finally asked.

"Well . . . this one is a little weird."

"How so?" Brisbane prompted.

"The car was found crashed in a gulley. But no one was there. The car was abandoned, it seems. So the officer who called it in said it was suspicious."

Suspicious? Rylie never could dismiss anything that sounded suspicious. Especially since it involved the Highway Thru Hell. "Hmm . . ." she said.

"Are you thinking what I'm thinking?" Brisbane asked.

"I doubt that." They were just too different. "But I think we should go check it out. If it's suspicious, it might have something to do with one of the other crimes."

He nodded and handed her the keys, and they headed for the door. "For the record, that's exactly what I was thinking."

## CHAPTER FOUR

This time, Rylie was thankful that Brisbane didn't eat his pistachios. Instead, he sat in the passenger seat of her truck, leafing through the files of the kidnapping victims. But when she glanced over, she quickly found something else to grouch at. She wasn't in a particularly grouchy mood—in fact, she felt pretty good—but Brisbane just made it so *easy*.

"Uh . . . Bris?" she said, using the nickname she'd heard Beeker call him. "Watch what you're doing?"

"Hmm?" he said, staring hard at the paper. "*No sign of struggle.*"

That was another pet peeve of hers. People who couldn't read to themselves in their head and had to move their lips and say things aloud. She pointed. "Could you look at what you're doing? You're smudging the papers with your grubby fingers."

He glanced up at the red smears. "Oh. Darn. Sorry."

He started to lick them, which was even worse. She reached into the console and pulled out a pack of wet wipes, tossing them to him.

"Thanks," he said, using one. As he wiped his fingers, he checked her speedometer. "Going a little fast there, are we?"

She glanced down. Of course *he* thought so—he drove like an old lady. But she was pushing one-hundred. Even for her, that was a little too fast. She eased off the gas. "Just want to get there."

Brisbane nodded, satisfied. "All these girls were last seen on the interstate, near the Montana-Wyoming border. But judging from where the bodies of the two girls were found—a considerable distance away from the highway—it means that we may never find them."

"Yeah. I thought about that. That one girl's body was found near Tie Siding."

"Yeah. Where's that?"

"Wyoming. But nowhere near the interstate. I checked on the map."

He shook his head and let out a long breath. "I wonder if this Gary guy has any connection to that place."

"Probably. The guy who picked up Nina Maxwell was likely a Wyoming native. He talked to her pretty knowledgably about rodeos, right? And she said he seemed to know the area. So I don't think he was a transient. Either that, or he was a former truck driver. So I think it's looking more and more like this Gary Vinton guy. He checks all our boxes."

Rylie had been going ninety, but she laid off the gas when she saw the patrol cars in the distance. The crash was only about five miles from the Buffalo town limits. She pulled to the side of the road, behind one of the patrol cars. Before she could get out, Brisbane let out a long whistle.

"What?" she asked, following his line of vision. But from her vantage point, she couldn't see anything more than a broken guardrail. She craned her neck. The asphalt was covered with black tire marks, skidding toward the side of the road, and the grass on the other side of the railing had been rutted.

"Would you look at that."

"I can't see anything," she said, hastily pulling off her seatbelt and rushing to the side of the road. When she was there, she saw just what Brisbane meant.

The Chevy Silverado was nearly vertical, headlights down, in a deep, dry gully. "Wow," she said, moving closer. As she did, an officer joined her.

"Hey, you guys are gonna need to get back in your car and move on," he said warily, hooking his thumbs through his belt loops. "This ain't the place for sight-seeing."

Rylie pulled out her credentials. "We're from the FBI. We got word from the state police up the road that this might have been suspicious?"

"Oh, geez," the guy said, his voice cracking. "How do you do?"

"Fine . . .," Rylie stared at him, waiting for him to answer the question, but he seemed flustered, so she checked the gold name badge on his breast and prompted, "Officer Lyons, this crash? You're the one who called it in, yes? Why did you think it was suspicious?"

He cleared his throat. "Oh! Yeah. We did because, well . . . no driver."

"No driver?"

"Yeah, well, obviously there was a driver there, once. And she left her cell phone in there, purse, and a bunch of cash," he continued. "But she got out of the car and who knows where she went? We never received any call from her. We got a call from a traveler who'd pulled to the side of the road to take a break, and saw the skid marks on the road."

She climbed over the guardrail and tried to walk down the fairly steep incline.

As she did, he followed her close behind. "Yeah, like I said. I'm Jeff Lyons. I've been in the police up here for six years, right out of high school. It's been my dream to join the FBI. I submit my application every year but it keeps getting turned down. How'd you get in?"

The question hung out there, unanswered. Rylie had no intention of rehashing the events that led her to doggedly pursue the FBI, because she knew she'd wind up thinking about her family. So she simply let the time stretch out as she stood halfway down the incline, studying the truck from a new angle. It was an old Chevy Silverado, probably from the 1990s, but other than being half-swallowed by the gully, the back side of the trailer was in fairly good shape. The tires looked new, and it was shiny, as if someone had recently given it a good waxing.

"And how long has this truck been there, have you determined?"

"Uh. Just since last night." His tone was heavy with disappointment. He clearly wanted an answer to his question.

*Sorry. Not happening. Ask Mr. PR up there. He'd probably talk your ear off for so long, you'll regret asking.*

Rylie tried to climb down as gracefully as she could, but gravity took hold and she wound up running the rest of the way to the bottom of the gulch. The officer was right behind her. "And you said you found her purse? Who was she?"

"Her name was Lila Garrity. She's twenty-three. Lives in Sheridan. She works at the Bozeman Steakhouse in Buffalo."

"Bozeman?" Brisbane called from the road above. "That place is great."

She would've rolled her eyes at him, but she was too interested in knowing more. "You make a call to the local police in Sheridan?"

"Sure did. And yeah. Her husband had reported her missing this morning. He said she was coming home from a shift at the steakhouse and had called him on the road. At that point, everything was just fine."

Rylie moved to the edge of the gully and looked closer. The front of the truck had been flattened like the bellows of an accordion. She moved to the edge of the dusty gully and crouched in the dirt to peer in the driver's side door, which was about halfway open. The airbag had been deployed and there were a few dollar bills and change on the frame of the open door, plus a dark ruddy substance that was likely dried blood on the inside door handle.

She scanned the dirt outside the door and saw several male footprints with a diamond shape in the center. "Officer?"

He'd been resting against a rock, but rushed to her side. "Yes, ma'am? Uh, agent?"

"Can I see your shoe?"

"My . . . ?" He looked down, confused, at his scuffed black uniform shoes.

"Your sole."

Balancing on one foot, he tried twice to lift the shoe to show her the sole, but he fell over each time. The second time, though, she managed to catch the shape of a diamond before he toppled. "One second," he said, stooping to untie it.

"Forget it," she said, letting out a sigh. Of course, the crime scene was contaminated. These small-town cops weren't prepared for major crimes. The officer had likely just believed he'd come across the scene of an abandoned truck.

But who abandoned a truck and left her purse, her cell phone, and all her money? Rylie had a feeling that it was much more than that.

As she turned to leave, she noticed a couple of deep ruts, about the width of a female heel. They trailed off from the gully's embankment a few yards before disappearing.

A shadow fell over her. "Anything?"

She looked up. Brisbane had finally joined her. "Yeah. What does this look like to you?"

He stooped. "She was dragged?"

Rylie shrugged. "That's what it looks like to me. Can't be sure, though."

"Dragged?" Officer Lyons asked, wide-eyed. "No kidding? You guys are good."

Brisbane peered in the window, too, then moved closer. He was tall enough to reach across the divide and nudge the airbag out of the way. "That's definitely blood."

Sure enough, with the bag pushed away, she had a better view of a large smear of blood, probably from a palm print. She looked at Lyons. "We're going to want to get prints here."

"Oh, yeah. Sure." The officer nodded as she backed away from the scene. Then he said, "Pretty weird, huh? But I bet you guys see all kinds of weird things."

She decided to leave Brisbane to answer that one, since he loved to chatter. He was much better at the inevitable social part of the job, which entailed playing nice with the people they came across who were curious about their job. Making small talk, engaging in public relations to enhance the FBI's image. And he came through. "Sure do. I can tell you some pretty wild stories."

Lyons must've sensed an "in" with Brisbane, because he started again. "I've always wanted to be an FBI agent. How'd you--"

Brisbane leaned over and picked something out of a scraggly bush. He held it up. "Piece of fabric."

Rylie came to his side. "We should find out what uniform they use at Bozeman's. See if it matches the victim's clothing."

"I can do that for you," Officer Lyons said. "Pretty crazy, that she'd crash and someone would drag her off, huh? But that ain't even the weirdest part."

Rylie had started to walk back up the embankment, hardly listening to the officer, but at those words, she stopped short. Turned, waiting for the punchline. But Officer Lyons just stood there, grinning like a cat toying with a canary before he swallows it.

"What's the weirdest part?" she prompted.

The young officer twisted his hands in front of him, pausing too long for dramatic effect. Just as Rylie was about to tell him to spit it out, he said, "Just that it's the second abandoned vehicle we've found around here in as many days."

"What was the first?" Brisbane asked, echoing her thoughts.

"It was a mile or so down the road, on the other side of the highway," he explained, pointing down the road. "The car belonged to a girl who'd just been passing through, driving alone. She crashed it on the side of the road, same as here. One-car accident. And then she just up and disappeared."

Rylie blinked. Another crash? She glanced at Brisbane, who looked similarly interested in the news. "You have details on that crash?"

"Not myself. I didn't look into it. But I can get them for you, if you want to come with me back to my station?"

"Yes, thanks," she said, turning to head back up the embankment.

"Hey, Wolf," Brisbane called from behind her. "Look at this."

She whirled to find him back near the truck, but on the other side of the gully. How he'd gotten there, she had no idea. She followed to the other side of the gully and said, "What?"

"Come here."

She gauged the distance. It was probably a good ten feet across. "You may have been blessed with long legs, but I haven't been."

"Oh, come on." He grinned playfully. "Just take a running start and long-jump it."

She glared at him, then started to back up. "This better be worth it."

"It is. Promise."

*Good, because if you are asking me to come over there as a joke, I will strangle you with my belt.*

She took that running start, pumping her arms and legs, and when she reached the edge of the gully, leapt with every ounce of power she had. To her surprise, she easily sailed over the gap, landing gracefully on her feet on the other side and running until she skidded to a stop.

Behind her, she heard Brisbane applauding, with a slow, teasing golf-clap. When she turned, he was smiling. "Nice form. I give it an eight point nine."

"Shut up. What?" she asked, coming closer.

He was standing beside the truck, staring at its back-end, which, because it was buried in the gully, came to Brisbane's nose-height. Rylie saw what had interested him at once.

The truck that had looked so well-kept from the other side had recently been into a little fender bender. The taillight had been smashed, the chrome fender dented.

"Another car hit this truck," she murmured.

"Yep. But that's not all." He pointed at the fender.

She ran a finger over it and squinted to get a better look. Black paint.

Just like the truck that Gary Vinton drove.

"You think whoever hit the car might've taken Lila Garrity?" Brisbane asked.

"That's a good assumption," she said, standing up and jumping easily back across the gap. "I wonder if the same thing happened with that other car. Let's get IDs on that first victim, start digging into the file, and see what we can find."

# CHAPTER FIVE

Sheldon Weibel stepped out of the white school bus for the Wyoming Correctional Center and took his first breath of freedom in over six months.

Well, not *actual* freedom. In a few hours, he'd be shuttled back into the prison to continue the rest of his one-year-stint within its dank walls.

But now, he savored the taste of the air on his tongue—it was different from the air in the outside recess yard. With sixty other inmates crowded around him, the air of that place was always thick with body odor and blacktop and the garbage from whatever slop they'd tried to feed them that day.

No, this was what the world was supposed to be. The breeze was fresh and earthy, metallic and cold, smelling slightly of the fresh laundry Valerie used to bring in from the backyard line. And he couldn't wait to get back to it.

*Seven more months,* he said to himself, following the line of inmates to the back of the bus and picking up his trash bag.

It was bullshit, the reason he was here. When he and Valerie had broken up, he'd taken her car. He knew she'd be pissed, but what he hadn't known was that the car had been lifted by Valerie's ex, six months prior. So, because he'd had a rap sheet a mile long, the judge had thrown the book at him. Back to the Wyoming Correctional Center for him.

Even before that, though, at forty, he'd been getting tired of this hamster wheel. Wanting to make something of himself. Have a girl. A family. That was why he was with Valerie. He saw himself married to her. He'd wanted to propose, and then she'd gone and cheated on him.

After that, it had all gone wrong.

Seven more months, and he'd be free again. And this time, he wouldn't screw it up. After all, what had Father Beam said at last Sunday's sermon? *It's never too late . . . until it is.*

He wandered down the side of the road, picking up an old cigarette sleeve, checking to see if there were any inside, then tossing it into the bag.

It wasn't too late. He was only forty. Father Beam said he had plenty of time to start over. Turn over that proverbial new leaf.

And he would.

He'd try, at least.

"Hey, Weibel!" a voice called behind him as he stooped over the guardrail to pick up a plastic cup from the other side.

He glanced back, raising his hand to shield his face. Gallagher. The brown-nosing snot. He was always giving him trouble. He twirled his bully stick and raised his hands, palms up, to the sky. "What are you doing?"

"I was just . . ."

He'd gotten too far away from them. That was probably what Gallagher would say. *Wait up. Where do you think you're going?* He was used to the corrections officers breathing down his neck. But Gallagher was the biggest snot of all of them.

"Well, you're not doing a very good job, whatever it is," he said with a guffaw. "Look at that trash down there! That escape your attention?"

Weibel lumbered toward the edge of the guardrail and looked over. Sure enough, it looked like someone had broken open a bag full of someone's Hardee's dinner, all over the place. Napkins, Styrofoam, white paper, straws, ketchup packets—they were strewn across the tall grass.

He let out a groan and looked around, trying to figure out how to get down there. He wiped the sweat from his bald head, which was leaking into his eyes, despite the chill in the air. The slope was pretty steep and with his bum leg, he couldn't do much.

The other guys were coming closer. Gallagher snapped at him, "Come on. Get a move on. We don't have all day."

Taking a breath, Weibel threw a leg over the guardrail, straddling it. Then he pushed himself over and headed down the slope. He had to grab handfuls of the grass to anchor himself so that he didn't fall, but eventually he made it down without stumbling.

Then he started to pick up the pieces of trash, stuffing them into his bag. Every month, this opportunity came up, and every month, he'd been passed over, to his disappointment. But now, he had to wonder why he'd been so excited. It hardly seemed worth it. Part of him would've rather been back in his cell. *Work release used to be a lot more fun,* he thought, *Before this jerk-wad, Gallagher.*

As he squatted to pick up an empty French fry sleeve, slightly nostalgic for the way a McDonald's fry would taste, warm and salty and straight out of the drive-thru, he noticed it.

Something sky-blue, caught between the limbs of a nearby bush.

The color was off. It wasn't from nature. It had to be a piece of garbage.

A big one, too. He looked at his bag. It was nearly full. He probably didn't have enough room for whatever it was.

Letting out a grunt, he lumbered over to it, dragging his bum foot across the uneven ground. He shoved aside branches to reveal the pile of rags, gauging the size of the thing, deciding that yes-- he'd definitely need a new bag.

*And that jerk-wad Gallagher is going to make me go up and get it myself, I bet you.*

The moment the thought entered his mind, he pushed aside another branch and saw a pair of dark brown eyes, staring at him.

He jumped back and let out a yelp.

Gallagher called to him, annoyed. Something like, "Hurry up and get your fat ass moving, Weibel!"

But Weibel couldn't be bothered. He moved closer to take in those eyes. They belonged to a girl with long dark hair, a button nose, bow lips. Her face was smudged with dirt. Her limbs were folded beneath her, her blue top ripped to expose more pale gray flesh than it should have. She was so young. So beautiful. And dead.

Weibel's hands shook as he brought them to his heart, cupping it to stop it from beating out of his chest.

*It's never too late . . . until it is.*

He let out a mournful wail and fell to his knees.

## CHAPTER SIX

Rylie followed the young police officer into the tiny break room in the back of their cramped, two-person station. “This is fine,” she said.

Officer Lyons removed his hat and blushed. “It’s not much. I’m sorry.”

The poor guy’s ears were bright red from the embarrassment. He’d been more than happy to welcome the two FBI agents back to his local police station, but he seemed intent on apologizing for everything about it.

Brisbane clapped him on the back. “It’s okay. Don’t worry about it.”

“I bet you have pretty fancy digs at the FBI, huh?” he continued, hovering in the doorway.

“Not really,” Brisbane said with a shrug.

That was an understatement. The new Rapid City Field office had been the old home of the South Dakota SPCA. Their cubicles were practically cages, with high, chain-link walls. She’d only learned that after a couple of days of working there, when she wondered out loud why the place constantly smelled like wet dog.

She moved a plastic chair close to the folding table and sat down. “Officer. . . can you get us whatever you have in your files for the two missing girls?”

“Sure thing,” he said, running off.

Brisbane watched him go and laughed. “You sure know how to scare a guy.”

“What does that mean?”

“Nothing. Just that I think he’s reconsidering his life’s goal of being in a Fed, after meeting you. You’re not one for small talk.”

“Small talk wastes time.” She crossed her arms. “Besides, I can’t help it. I want things when and how I want them. And I can’t help thinking that we’re wasting time with small talk when we can be helping these girls.”

“I get it. I get it,” he mumbled, though she wasn’t sure he did. He went to the coffee service and poured two cups of the steaming liquid.

He handed one to her. Then, predictably, he stood in front of the vending machine, fishing through his pockets.

She didn't have to wonder what he was looking for. She reached into her purse and pulled out a dollar bill. "Here."

"Thanks, Buddy," he said, grinning at her as he took it.

"Anything to get you to concentrate on the reason we're here," she grumbled, taking a sip. Surprisingly, it wasn't bad.

"Well, it might have been this Vinton character. But with the girls missing, there's not much we can do. I hate to say it, but we'd have better luck if we found a body," he said, pressing a button.

*Found a body.* She winced at the thought of her best friend, Kiki, in her braids and white flowered sundress, lying in a pool of her own blood. Shot twice in the head, execution-style.

She didn't care how much it would help. She *never* wanted to find a body.

The machine thumped. He reached in and pulled out a Snickers, unwrapped it, and offered her the bar. "Bite?"

"No," she said, looking up at the bulletin board. There were postings for the Annual Policeman's Ball, some quilt sale going on in the VFW, and the FBI Most Wanted, along with a flyer with bottom phone-number tear-aways for a local housecleaning service. "But here's what I'm thinking. That Vinton guy has been really making the rounds. Causing an accident last night, then picking up a hitchhiker this morning?"

Brisbane sat down across from her and tore off a bite with his teeth that was half the bar. "Busy guy," he said between chews, putting his ankle on his other knee and drumming a hand on the table. "Sounds like he really has an obsession with pretty young girls. One he can't control."

She frowned. "That's the thing. Vinton's past sounded so normal, didn't it? In the file, there were a couple of women who dated him and said he was a little creepy, a little handsy. But he'd never even had a parking ticket. He followed the law. For him to confess to murdering hitchhikers to Clive, then to go around kidnapping girls in broad daylight . . . it's a little bit of a stretch."

"Hey. That's what everyone thought about Ted Bundy. Nice guy . . ."

"But eventually, Ted Bundy's past caught up with him."

"And if Gary Vinton is our guy, his past will catch up with him, too. He can't get away with this forever."

She tried to be comforted by that thought, but she simply couldn't be. Michael didn't know the skeletons in her closet. He didn't know that someone *had* gotten away with murdering her mother, best friend, and best friend's mother, and kidnapping her sister, twenty years ago. Every time she tried to tell herself that she'd find her guy, eventually, that thought always invaded. Sometimes, killers were just too smart, too good at evading authorities.

Try as she might, some killers would always get away.

She only hoped this case didn't prove to be one of those.

"Yeah, I guess," she said, as Lyons appeared, arms loaded with folders.

"All right, now we are in business," he said, piling the folders onto the table. "I've got a whole folder of information on Erin Littlefeather, the girl who disappeared yesterday. Not much yet on the new case, but I'm putting together my report. Anyway, Erin Littlefeather's dad is coming in. He lives down the street and he's the one who reported her missing. You want to talk to him?"

Brisbane nodded and popped the rest of his Snickers in his mouth. "Super, Lyons. Thanks. You're the best of the best, man."

Officer Lyons beamed in appreciation, then noticed him crumpling the wrapper. "Oh, Geez. The Chief isn't in right now but I called him when you two showed. He said I could use his credit card and buy us lunch, if you're interested."

Rylie didn't have to answer. Brisbane was all over that. "Yeah. That would be great. What places you have around here?"

Lyons started to rattle off names of fast-food restaurants in the area, as Rylie pulled the folder toward her. She opened it up to a picture of a girl with warm brown eyes and an infectious smile. It looked like it had been taken from a yearbook, because the girl was wearing a cheerleading uniform for Big Horn High School.

A sick feeling swelled in Rylie's gut. Didn't matter what the girl looked like—every time she saw a picture of a young female, she thought of Maren.

"Steak," Brisbane concluded. "You got any menus from places?"

Lyons opened a drawer and scattered them on the table along with the files. Rylie pushed away a brochure for a place called Pizza Heaven and said, "Hey, Bris. Look at this."

He looked up from a brochure. "What?"

"This girl, Erin, was seventeen. Her car was found right outside the exit for the town of Banner. One car crash. There were footprints leading out from the wreckage so the police and her family thought that she might've hitched a ride to the hospital or taken herself to the local medical center, but no one's seen her."

He lifted the folder and stared at it. "Doesn't say whether there was damage indicative of another car being involved."

Just then, there was the sound of the front door opening, outside. "Hello?" a voice asked.

Lyons stuck his head out into the hallway, glancing toward the front desk. Then he said, "Dick Littlefeather is here."

Rylie jumped up, and the three of them went to the reception area. Dick Littlefeather was a short, stocky man with more than a few wrinkles on his countenance. He was wearing a cowboy hat, barn jacket, and dust-covered jeans.

"Mr. Littlefeather," Lyons said, shaking his head. "Good to see you. I'd like to introduce you to two FBI agents, Rylie Wolf and Michael Brisbane. They're going to help you get your daughter back."

*Well, we're going to try,* Rylie qualified in her head. *As best we can . . .*

The father shook their hands, bowing slightly. "Thank you. Thank you so much . . ."

The praise was so effusive, Rylie felt the need to cut him off right away. After all, they hadn't done anything yet. "Yes. Mr. Littlefeather. Can you tell me a little about your daughter, Erin? Where was she headed?"

"She was coming home from visiting the Ghost," he explained.

"The . . . Ghost?" Brisbane asked.

"Devil's Tower," Lyons put in. "You know. That big butte out to the east of us? From *Close Encounters of the Third Kind?"*

"Oh . . .," Rylie said, understanding now. "That's pretty far away. She went to the Ghost often by herself?"

He nodded. "She knows the way like her own home. We are Lakota. In our tribe, it is common for our people to go to the Ghost to seek wisdom and guidance, to seek enlightenment. Erin often went there for answers. For solitude."

"Ah," Rylie said, nodding. "Was there something troubling her?"

"No. Nothing more than the usual thing that would be bothering a teenage girl. She was concerned about choosing a college. She knew it was a big decision. I think she went for answers to that," he said, shaking his head. "It is not like her to go off and leave without any notice to me."

"When was the last time you spoke to her?"

"Yesterday morning, when she made it to the Ghost. I saw her off that morning. Then she called me to tell me she'd gotten there safe, would spend a few hours there, and be home by dinner. I did not worry. She was a good driver." He shook his head sadly. "But when she didn't come home . . ."

Rylie looked at Brisbane, wondering if he was thinking what she was thinking. Unless Erin had gotten held up, it meant the accident had happened in the daylight. If her car was driven off the road by the kidnapper, that meant he'd taken a big risk.

She looked at the officer. "And you've called all the medical centers around the area?"

Dick Littlefeather spoke up. "I did. I did that even before I contacted the police. I had a strong feeling, when she wasn't home for dinner, that something was wrong, so I started calling around. And when I came up empty, I called the authorities to report her missing."

Lyons nodded. "Officer Grant found her car a little after six o'clock, last night. At the Story Creek exit."

She blinked. "Story Creek?" She swallowed, forcing back memories that threatened to invade. "I thought the file said it was the exit for Banner?"

"Yeah." He looked at her. "Story Creek, Banner. Same difference."

*Story Creek.* She hadn't heard the name of that town in decades.

Her mouth opened, and at first, nothing came out. "There's an old RV campsite out there, isn't there?"

"Nah, there's not much of anything out there," Lyons said with a shake of the head. "Well, there used to be one there, before I was born. But there were a bunch of murders there, from what I hear. Shut the place down real quick. No one wants to hook up at a damn graveyard."

Rylie stiffened. *A bunch of murders.* He said it so cavalierly, as if it hadn't destroyed two families in one single blink of an eye.

She took a deep breath. Blew it out. By then, she knew Brisbane was staring curiously at her. *Get it together, Rylie.*

She shook the father's hand. "All right. Thank you. We will be in touch if we find anything."

He sniffled a little and once again thanked her profusely. "I know you will do everything you can to bring her home."

"That's the plan," Brisbane said, putting a comforting hand on his shoulder as he walked him to the door. "We'll keep you up to date."

After the father left, he turned to her. “We should go check out the site of the accident, huh?”

“No,” she said instantly, memories swarming her. “No . . . not yet . . .”

He raised an eyebrow at her. “Why n—"

“Later,” she said emphatically, turning away, thinking, *Never.*

As she moved down the hall, the image of her own father planted itself in her head. He’d been standing in confusion at the front door when she’d arrived in the back of the police car after the worst event of her life. The police had given her a teddy bear and told her to wait there, so she’d watched, through the rain-spattered back window, twisting that poor bear in her hands.

She’d never forget his wide eyes, his wobbling voice as he first asked, then screamed, for someone to tell him what the hell was going on. When Rylie had finally come out of the back of the car, he’d hugged her so tight, she thought he’d crush her.

Littlefeather had the same look about him, as if he was teetering on the edge of insanity. His life had been torn away from him in an instant. The first time she’d seen her father, with those tears in his eyes, she would’ve done anything to turn back time and take all the pain away from him. But nothing could be done.

Here, though, there was still a chance. If there was a possibility for a happy ending, she had to find it.

So she would try.

But she’d go near Story Creek, as a last resort, only if she *had* to.

She picked up her pace back to the cramped break room and flipped through the crime scene photographs, her eyes landing on something, almost at once. “Bris!”

He burst into the doorway, skidding to a stop as if he’d run there. “What? What’s wrong?”

“Look,” she said, showing him a photograph of the car.

It was an old car, a tomato-red Dodge Dart. But on the rear side panel, there was a dent. And, unmistakably, a smear of black paint.

“Holy cow,” Brisbane breathed. “So it was—”

“Guys,” Lyons called, appearing in the doorway, looking just as shell-shocked as they felt, which was strange, because he hadn’t seen the photograph yet.

“What’s the problem?” Rylie said, sure it wasn’t as important as her latest discovery. Because this was huge. She looked at Brisbane, ready to complete his thought. "It means that the two disappearances are connect—"

"Guys. That was patrol officer Gregg. He just radioed in."

She stopped and looked at the officer. Was he going to pause for dramatic effect again? "And?"

"And they just found a body. Out near the Sheridan town limits."

Rylie closed her eyes. It was news, but not the news she'd wanted to hear. When she lifted herself to standing, her knees wobbled. "All right. Let's go."

## CHAPTER SEVEN

There was a great commotion at the site of the body's discovery. About a half a mile before they arrived there, Rylie saw the orange, flag-adorned road signs, stating *LITTER REMOVAL- NEXT 2 MILES.* A bit after that, they came across a white school bus for the Wyoming Correctional Center, filled with inmates in orange jumpsuits who leered at them as they passed. Not far from that, they found a police car, an ambulance, as well as a number of uniformed people.

Lyons had accompanied them to the scene. When Rylie pulled behind the police car, Lyons was right behind her. The second she stepped out, he led her toward the crowd, breaking through.

"Listen up, guys. FBI agents, coming through!"

They all turned to look at them, and the crowd parted.

Lyons clapped an older man with a leathered face and salt-and-pepper curls on the shoulder. "Agents. This is Gregg. The guy who was first on the scene. He called in the sighting."

"Thanks," Rylie said, shaking his hand. "I'm Rylie Wolf. So the corrections department alerted you to the body?"

"That's right," he said, his voice impossibly low. "This fella here, he found it."

He pointed to another man, extremely pear-shaped, with flyaway gray hair and doughy jowls covered in gray stubble. He was wearing an orange jumpsuit with grass stains on the knees. Unsmiling, he attempted a wave, but his hands had been cuffed in front of him.

"Your name?" Brisbane said, taking out his notepad.

"Weibel. Sheldon Weibel."

Rylie held up a finger and started to walk toward the edge of the road. She climbed over the guardrail, searching the area until she saw the yellow tape. "I want to see the body first. It's still there?"

He nodded. "We just finished taking photos of the scene. Waiting on the medical examiner."

She proceeded down the embankment, not waiting for permission, though she could feel Brisbane trailing behind her, his heavy footfalls matching her own. The body was back toward a line of skeletal trees and scrubby bushes. She stepped through the long grass and pushed aside the limbs of the bush to get a better look.

The girl's eyes were open, staring forever at nothing. They were deep brown, and her dark hair was splayed out, some of it caught on the branches surrounding her head. There was a single visible bruise on her throat, a trickle of blood from her pert nose, a bluish tinge to her skin, but other than that, she looked almost alive.

Rylie swallowed. She'd seen photographs of the girl, alive, in the file, just minutes ago.

It was Erin Littlefeather.

She looked away, surprised to find that Lyons and Gregg had also followed her. The next time she spoke, her voice was weak. "Do we know . . ." She cleared her throat so she wouldn't sound so affected. "You said the medical examiner's on his way? Do you have any idea the cause of death?"

The officer shrugged. "The bruising she has on her face could be from that car accident. But though there were a lot of footprints all around from the convicts, none of them were small enough to be hers. She has tiny feet. And if you look—she's barefoot."

Brisbane pushed aside a branch to confirm the fact. "So she was probably dumped here." He stooped closer. "Clothing's intact. No sign of sexual assault. Lot of bruises on her throat. My bet's on strangulation. What do you think?"

Rylie didn't want to look again. Her mind was cycling over an image of poor Dick Littlefeather. "Hmm . . . yeah," she said, heading back up to the roadside. Lyons was ahead of her. She asked, "Did the killer leave any evidence behind?"

"Not that our officers found. Maybe the medical examiner will find something."

Of course. It was too much to hope that this killer would let his obsession over young girls crowd his logical thinking, allowing him to leave evidence all over the crime scene. Once again, they were dealing with a criminal who was far too smart for that.

As she struggled to climb the embankment, Brisbane caught up with her. "You okay?"

The last thing she wanted was for her own weakness to show through. "Of course, why wouldn't I be?" she said immediately, shrugging off his hand when he offered it to her to help her up the steep incline.

She reached the prisoner, who was now sitting on a guardrail, flanked by a correction officer.

"Your name is, again . . .?"

"Sheldon Weibel," he said.

"Right." She vaguely remembered hearing him say that before. "You found the body . . . when?"

"'Bout an hour ago. I was just going through, picking up trash, and I seen something in the bushes. When I get there and move the branches around, I saw it was that young girl."

The corrections officer nodded. "We called it in right away. We didn't touch anything."

When she reached the top of the incline, another man had joined the group. Lyons said, "Agent. This is county medical examiner, Dr. Fred Barnes."

She shook his hand, dispensing with any small talk. "I'm pretty sure the victim is Erin Littlefeather, seventeen, who was reported missing last night," she said to him. As he started to walk away, she grabbed his arm. "Please, make your examination of this body a priority. We have reason to believe he may have abducted another girl, who might still be alive."

He nodded and said, "I'll have preliminary information right now. But we'll have to get the body to my office where I'll perform a thorough examination."

"How long will that take?"

He scratched his jaw. "Once I'm done here, two hours, maybe? When I'm finished, if you'd like, you're welcome to follow me over and wait."

"Yeah. We will." Rylie shivered, and hugged herself, once again thinking about Dick Littlefeather. The poor man would never be the same.

"You okay?"

She was roused from her thoughts by Brisbane, who, once again, was stooping a little to look into her eyes. "Yes," she said, turning away from him. "Stop asking me that."

"You just look a little rattled."

He had no idea. "I'm fine. I just want to get the information as quick as we can so that we can help Lila Garrity."

He nodded but didn't say more, which made her think he didn't believe her. She leaned against the railing and watched the medical examiner stoop over the body, in silence. After a moment, he looked up and called, “Definitely murder. From the looks of it, manual strangulation, likely by a male suspect.”

The EMTs lowered a stretcher down to transport the body as she glanced at Brisbane. “Gary Vinton,” she murmured.

“Maybe.”

She pushed away from the railing. “Let’s go with the medical examiner and see what else he comes up with.”

# CHAPTER EIGHT

Rylie sat in a stark waiting room in the basement of the Sheridan Medical Center, where Dr. Fred Barnes set up shop. A small television was droning in the corner, talking politics, something she had no interest in.

"Just another day of squabbling in D.C., huh?" Brisbane said. He'd been pacing the floor, pausing every so often to take a slurp from the Coke bottle he'd bought from the vending machine, but when he turned, he must've noticed her eyes on the television.

She rubbed her eyelid tiredly. "I don't know. I don't care. I don't pay attention to that stuff."

"You don't?" He laughed. "I don't know. I'm not a junkie or anything, but every so often I like to see what's going on, considering they sign our paychecks, you know?"

That was the last thing she wanted to think about. She wasn't even sure she'd gotten a paycheck since she left Seattle. All of her expenses, so far, had been reimbursed by the field office. She had much more pressing thoughts on her mind.

"Could you stop pacing?" she asked, looking up at him. "You're distracting me."

He sat down next to her, leaning back in the chair. Then he leaned forward suddenly and clamped a hand on her knee, to her shock.

Steadying it.

*Oh*, she thought. She'd been bouncing again. She always bounced her knee when she was nervous about something.

"*That* was distracting me," he said with a smirk.

She frowned and looked past the double doors to the morgue. A long hallway stretched beyond it. Empty. Where the hell was he?

"What do you think is taking so long?" she wondered.

He checked his phone. "It's only been an hour. He said—"

"Yes, but didn't I impress upon him how important it was to get this information right away? Lila Garrity might—"

"You did," he said, clamping a hand down on her knee once more. She'd been bouncing again. "But you know, sometimes, when someone says a task is going to take two hours to complete, it actually winds up taking two hours. And if he's worth his salt, he's not going to cut corners for an antsy FBI agent."

She sighed. He was probably right.

He moved to the edge of his seat. "If you have another dollar, I'll get you something to drink from the machine. Without caffeine, since you don't need it."

She shook her head. "I'm fine."

"Suit yourself," he said, then looked at his soda. "You wouldn't have a dollar for me? All I had today was that Snickers."

"You had nuts."

"Those don't count."

Sure, tell that to her poor truck. She glared at him, then reached for her purse. As she was rummaging through it, the double doors opened, and Dr. Barnes appeared, shaking his head and holding a folder in his hand as he walked at a purposeful clip toward them.

"Well?" she asked.

"Just as I said. Manual strangulation, male suspect likely. She had a number of abrasions and lacerations on her face and body, but most of them appear to be from the impact of the car accident. They were sustained quite a bit of time prior to her death."

Rylie nodded. "So she was taken somewhere after the accident and murdered later."

"Yes, it appears so, quite a bit later. I'd say up to ten hours later."

"Then he keeps them, for whatever reason, before disposing of them."

The medical examiner nodded. "Also—another point of note. She's missing a finger."

"A finger? Why do you think—"

"It's anybody's guess." He shrugged.

"Well, thank you." She looked at Brisbane. "If he murdered her several hours after the kidnapping, it means that if we're lucky, there's a chance Lila Garrity might still be alive."

Brisbane nodded. "Yeah. Stands to reason."

Ideas and possibilities teemed in Rylie's head. There were so many angles she could pursue. As she stood there, narrowing it down, Brisbane said, "What are you thinking?"

"I think we should go to the site of Erin Littlefeather's abduction, now," she said.

"You mean . . ."

She tried to say the words, *Story Creek,* but they tasted bitter on her tongue.

"Banner?" Brisbane filled in.

Right. It was called that, wasn't it? Even though it was off the same exit as the town of Banner, Story Creek, hopefully, was far away. Everything in Wyoming was far away from everything else. It was one of the benefits of living in Big Sky Country. Nothing was on top of you. You could really spread out, look for miles and miles in all directions and not see another sign of life.

"Right, Banner."

Maybe she wouldn't have to see the place of her biggest life tragedy, at all.

This time, even though she wasn't ready, she knew it had to be done. Like always, she would put her head down, concentrate on the task at hand, and push her way through it.

## CHAPTER NINE

It was coming.

Soon. But not yet.

Trying to put a lid on his excitement, the Scarred Man took a drag of his cigarette and gazed out the window, at the long expanse of untamed wilderness before him. Acres and acres of flat, dusty earth, dotted with creosote bushes, punctuated every so often by a butte or a slowly rising chocolate mountain, part of the Bighorn range. Orange cream clouds spread across the sky, crowning the setting sun.

His home. His beautiful home. To think, he'd locked himself away from this for so long.

The bitter wind slapped his face, and he tipped back his cowboy hat and let the last rays of the day's sunshine hit his face.

He smiled.

Well, he always smiled.

Even on the worst of his days, that grin was there. But today was a good day. A very good one.

Rubbing his rough chin, half five o'clock stubble, half mottled with scars, he turned to the rearview mirror. He tilted his face into the last orange rays of sun, letting them turn his face a fiery red. Freddy Krueger had nothing on him.

"You sure are a handsome little devil," he said aloud, sticking a toothpick between his permanently grinning lips.

That was something people never said about him. Handsome? Hell, no.

A freak? Yes, that was more like it.

When he was younger, it was bad enough that other kids would run away screaming. That he'd try to work up his courage to ask his crush out, only to be called Pizza Face by her and half her friends. That his teachers would whisper behind his back, *They should put that poor thing out of its misery.*

For a long time, he'd listened to them. After junior year in high school, he'd hidden himself away. Thought about ending it all. Prayed

God would take him in the night. He'd believed all those people were right, and that he didn't belong in this world.

But then his aunt stopped by with a stack of old comic books from one of his cousins.

And everything changed.

Finn Cooley, Firefly, Crossbones, Jigsaw . . . and of course, The Joker. All of them were mistreated by society for their hideous looks. But they had one thing in common—they didn't let their disfigurement get the best of them. They didn't curl up in a ball and feel sorry for themselves. The world wanted to shut them down, so they went and shut down the world.

He read page after page of those comics, until those characters were ingrained in his head. And he got to thinking, and he realized that hell—everyone had their faults. Their ugliness. It was more visible on some than on others. He had just as much right to walk the earth as any of them. Just as much right to look upon this Wyoming skyline. To breathe this air. To use this world's resources.

After what they put him through, he had even *more* of a right to it.

The wind died down for a second, and in that second, he heard the mournful whimper.

Pretty girl. She was awake.

Girls like her never had anything to worry about. They looked in the mirror in the morning and liked what they saw. People liked them, too. Stopped, took notice, and not to hurl insults at them or gape in disgust. No, it was for all good reasons. People tilted toward them like a flower to the sun, longed to be in their presence.

When they went out, people crowded them to pour affection on them. When they drove, they didn't have to obey the traffic signs. All girls like her had to do was flip that pretty long hair of theirs and bat those eyelashes, and the police would let them off, scot-free. It was a charmed life.

Girls like that were so stupid, they probably didn't even have to past their road tests. All they had to do was flirt a little with the tester, hike their skirts up, and they'd sail through with flying colors. When he'd gone for his test, the man had taken one look at him, then opened the door and vomited out the side of the car.

It wasn't fair.

But no one ever said life was. The Scarred Man knew this, better than anyone.

"There, there," he called out the window, mockingly, not caring if she heard his words of comfort. Then he added, under his breath, "*Bitch.*"

He started his truck and let it roar to life. Then he backed out, off the bluff, heading for the highway. This road was called the Highway Thru Hell, and he liked that. It sounded legendary, and he liked that he was a part of what had made it so hellish. Maybe one day, someone would write a comic book about him.

But right now, he had work to do. He'd take this pretty young thing to someplace remote, so that he could take his time, enjoy every last moment with her. Nights like this didn't last forever.

"Don't worry," he called to her as he pressed on the accelerator, his heart beating madly. It was not time yet, but it would be, soon. Once the sun went down and the millions of stars popped out in the velvet sky, she would meet her maker. "You're going to enjoy this so much, my love. Or at least, I will, but I hope you will, too."

His skin prickled with goosebumps as he thought of what was in store. He'd always imagined taking the life of someone who had wronged him—there had been many candidates for that over the years— but never thought it would bring such an inexplicable rush. The sheer excitement of it was far more than he'd anticipated. He'd known that the act of crushing a girl's windpipe would be extraordinary. Such a small action, barely any force at all, yet so devastating. Seeing her eyes, bulging and full of understanding that in her last moments on this earth, she would see him and only him. Feeling her smooth, perfect skin, alive, pulsing beneath his fingertips, only to slow to complete stillness. Touching the contours of her body as it grew cold and lifeless.

He glanced down at the newest cut on his forearm. It had scabbed over. A scratch, really, compared to the rest of him. He'd gotten it from the last one. She'd fought, hard. Scratched him with her fingernail.

That's why he'd had to cut it off. He couldn't have DNA everywhere, now, could he?

He had no idea how much that would excite him. He liked it when they struggled. It made it even more fun. He hoped this little girl, this blonde, would, too. She'd looked spunky, like a wild mustang, and he liked that.

He'd known another girl, like that, once. A long time ago.

*Bitch,* he thought bitterly.

His pulse skittered at the thought of giving this girl her due, dragging her out to the dusty Wyoming plain and making her pay. His breathing quickened. He couldn't wait to make it happen.

And he would do it, again and again, as much as he could, as long as he could.

This world was his, and he was its master.

Now, he needed to make up for lost time, for all those years he hid himself from the world, like a horrible secret. He'd take, and he'd take, and because it belonged to him, he wouldn't feel bad about it.

Not one bit.

# CHAPTER TEN

As Rylie drove closer and closer to Story Creek, she found herself drifting back to that day in the RV. She'd been sitting on one of the bunks beside the kitchen, watching Rose cook breakfast. The abundant sunshine framed her face, lighting up the flowered wallpaper and making everything bright and happy.

"You hungry, Ry?" Rose said, smiling up at her as she scraped scrambled eggs onto a plate. "Sleepy girl. You and Maren and Kiki must've stayed up way past your bedtime!"

She laughed, rubbing her eyes, and looked around. "Where are they?"

Maren was her older sister; Kiki was Rose's daughter. They'd been neighbors, and fast friends—almost like family. Rylie and Kiki had done everything together, so that was why Rose had invited her and her mom and Maren on a "Girls Trip" in their family RV that summer, tooling about the campsites around Yellowstone. It had been so fun, on the road, like a dream—driving most of the day, hooking up the campsite at night, drinking Cokes and margaritas while they sat by the fire and shared stories.

And then, everything had changed.

The always smiling, cherubic woman with the yellow curls looked to the window, and dropped the pan to the ground with a clatter. Hot oil spattered everywhere.

"Rylie," Rose warned, wiping her hands on her apron and heading for the door. "Go to the back bedroom now."

She scampered down from the bunk and froze there. Her parents always told her that the back bedroom was off-limits to kids. "But—"

"Do it! Now!" she shouted in a voice Rylie had never heard her use before.

More thunder boomed, and the earth shook with bright light, as if lightning had struck nearby. It spurred Rylie into action. Her skinny limbs working, she scrambled to the back of the RV and buried herself under the covers. Covered herself with blankets and prayed, even as she heard the door to the RV swinging open, and strange male voices, filling the space. "I thought there were three?" one had said.

"Naw. Just those two."

She wasn't sure what that had meant. Three young girls? Whatever the mistake was, it had saved her life. The door had slammed, and after that, there'd been nothing.

Nothing for hours and hours. Or at least, it seemed like that. Rylie had been bathed in sweat by the time she'd pulled herself out from her hiding spot. She'd crept to the dirt-crusted window over the RV's kitchenette sink and stared out at the bodies, lying motionless in a circle.

But no Maren. Maren was gone.

She'd stood over the bodies of the three females and sobbed her heart out. And then . . .

"Hey, whoa!" Brisbane said suddenly from the front passenger seat.

She blinked. "What's wrong?"

He motioned. "The exit."

Sure enough, they were coming up to it. She quickly swerved over the median and managed to take it.

He stared at her. "You sure you're all right?"

"Never better," she said, managing a smile as she came to the T-intersection at the end of the ramp. Sure enough, other than a faded sign that pointed to the left for Banner, the right for Story Creek, there was no trace of the Story Creek she remembered, at all. Just highway and yellow grass, stretching to a line of distant buttes. She refused to look any closer, instead concentrating on the top of her steering wheel. "Why?"

"Because your speed was falling off," he said. "You were going sixty. I was almost starting to feel comfortable with your driving."

"Ha. Ha," she mumbled. Had she really been going that slowly in an 80? And she'd been making fun of *him* for driving like an old lady. "Do we know where the Littlefeather girl's car was found?"

"Yep." He motioned for her to turn left. She gladly obliged, since it took her away from her nightmares. "Are you sure you're okay? Because you looked a little distracted."

When it was in her rearview mirror, she glanced back at the desolate road once, and collected herself. "How many times are you going to ask me that? For the last time, I'm fine!"

"All right, all right, sorry," he said in surrender, and immediately, she felt bad. He was the type of guy who noticed when people were hurting, and wanted to make things better. Meaning, the opposite of her. It wasn't that she didn't care—it was just that her mind was too preoccupied with other things to notice. But Michael Brisbane was different from her. "Hang a right, here."

The second she did, she saw the yellow tape marking off the place where the first car had come to rest. It was quite a ways off from 86, a place marked by a few scattered ponderosa pine and a large sign for a local mining company. "So she wasn't actually driving on the interstate when it happened?"

She remembered reading that in the report, but his nod confirmed it. "Yeah, she'd probably just exited, and was on her way home. She lives in Banner."

She pulled to the side of the road. The car was no longer there, but she'd seen pictures, so she could recreate the accident in her head. The girl, Erin Littlefeather, pulling off the highway, anxious to get home after her long trip. Maybe she didn't even notice the truck behind her until it was too late. He'd batted the back of her car, forcing her to lose control.

She followed the black skid marks that trailed off the road, to the car's final resting place. There were jewels of broken glass, but the earth was so hard, barely any ruts or tire tracks in it at all. Because there was nothing to stop it, the car had gone off quite a distance into the empty field, before colliding with a large metal sign that said Property of the Eagle Butte Coal Mine. Unlike the car, the sign had only a few scratches on it.

Rylie walked up and down the site, searching for any evidence, but there was nothing. "We have the police looking for that black truck, right? Any word?"

He shook his head. "So far, nothing."

Her lips twisted. "It shouldn't be so hard to find. Hardly anyone lives out here."

"But everyone and their mother owns a pick-up truck," he replied.

That was true. When she'd lived here, they'd been a pick-up truck family. That's why she'd bought one of her own, living in Seattle. She'd argued with her old boyfriend, Jim, about it—he wanted her to get a gas-efficient hybrid, but she'd quickly nixed that idea. There was a belief that you weren't really driving unless you were in a pick-up. Something about the ruggedness of it, the way the truck handled. It was one of the few things she still had in common with people out here.

“Well, this isn’t very helpful, now, is it?” she sighed as they walked back to the truck.

As she was getting in, she heard Brisbane’s phone, buzzing in his pocket. He fished it out and looked at the display. “It’s Lyons,” he said, picking up. “Brisbane here.”

*Why didn’t he call me?* she wondered, but only for half a second. Brisbane was the social one. She wasn’t.

“Uh-huh. Yeah,” he said, then paused. “Really?”

That sounded interesting. “What?”

He covered the mouthpiece with his hand. “We have a hit on that black truck. Another hitchhiker was just picked up outside of Banner. But she was savvy and jumped out before he could take off.”

“Banner . . . it’s not far away then . . .?”

“No. Let’s go. The guy can’t be too far away.”

She started the car and began to take off toward the town of Banner, even before he’d pulled his door shut. As he closed it, he spoke into the receiver, “Lyons, see if you can get someone to—” He paused. “Okay.”

Rylie floored it, the truck picking up dust on the side of the road. They sped through the cloud of it, toward the setting sun. “What’d he say?”

“He said he’s on his way right now. Some officers from Banner are in pursuit, too. But that the guy was headed east from Banner on 87, toward the interstate. Which means—”

“Which means he could be headed right toward us.”

“Right. So let’s go get him.”

She pressed harder on the gas, the world around her blurring as they sped off into the Powder River Basin.

# CHAPTER ELEVEN

Rylie's hands tightened around the steering wheel and she leaned forward in her seat. The sun had already sunk behind the Bighorn mountains, making it more difficult to see. She flipped on her headlights and squinted as far as she could see. The road seemed to disappear into the forest up ahead. There were no lights, coming toward them.

"Are you sure the guy's on this road?"

Brisbane wrapped his fingers around the door handle and braced himself. "I don't know anything. He could've turned off and gone anywhere."

"You said that the local police were in pursuit, right? Where are they?"

He snorted. "I'm not a psychic." He grabbed his phone and punched in a call. "Hey. Lyons. Where are you?"

He put it on speaker just as Lyons croaked, "I'm on eighty-seven. Just got off the interstate. The boys are on the Big Horn Highway, proceeding east."

"Great, well, that's really helpful," she said, looking around. It wasn't like any of these roads, though few, had street signs. Her headlights illuminated a sign that said, *Welcome to Banner.* "We're just getting into the town limits and we see nothing. Where, exactly, in relation to Banner?"

"It's south. He's heading south."

She peered at the GPS map on her dashboard. They were approaching Banner from the north. "We've got to get south," she muttered.

At that instant, she saw a crossroads. She braked too abruptly, so suddenly her head was thrown forward and back against the headrest. She quickly hung a left, tires screeching underneath her.

"Uh, Wolf? A little warning next time?" her partner said next to her. "I think I left my stomach back there."

She didn't answer. The tension was too high. The killer was on the run. And they could end it here, right now. But they had to get there.

This road wasn't paved. It was all dirt, and full of ruts. Instead of slowing down, she sped up, bouncing over the uneven terrain. Faster, faster . . . until . . .

"You know what I'm wondering?" Brisbane said, stiffly holding on for dear life. His fingernails dug into the center console, and he refused to take his eyes from the road.

"What?" she snapped. She didn't want to wonder. She wanted to *act*.

"What this means for Lila Garrity. If he's already trying to pick up another girl."

Her stomach sunk like a rock. She hadn't thought about it, but Brisbane was right. He wouldn't be trying to pick up a girl if he still had Lila to deal with. Or maybe he would be. "Maybe he's keeping Lila somewhere else. I hope."

"Yeah. But—"

"Look!" she shouted, sliding to the edge of her seat as she saw the lights of a police car, careening through the night in pursuit of a black pick-up. It was on the road directly in front of them, heading straight in the direction of the interstate.

She floored the gas pedal, sensing Brisbane wincing next to her. The police car sailed right past them in pursuit, and she spun the steering wheel, trying to join in. It was only when she got closer that she realized there was a median.

"Hold on."

"I am, believe me, I am."

They flew over the median with relative ease and she sailed onto the road, quickly coming up right behind the police officer. She passed him with little effort, gaining ground on the black truck ahead of her. His brake lights flickered on as he reached the on-ramp for the interstate. She didn't even tap her brakes.

"Uh, you might want to—" Brisbane said through gritted teeth. "Slow."

But she couldn't even think of the word. She was gaining on him. She punched the gas harder, willing her truck to go faster as she accelerated up the ramp, closing the gap between her truck and the suspect's. The engine roared underneath her as she reached the top of the ramp and surged ahead.

After a few moments, they were on his tail. She swerved into the fast lane to go around him. "Pit maneuver?" she asked him.

"No!" he shouted back. "Too high a speed. You'll kill us all."

“Then what?” she asked, as she pulled up so that their front windows lined up. The guy was staring ahead, intent, as if they weren’t there at all.

Brisbane motioned to the guy to pull over. He powered down the window and pointed. “Pull over! Pull . . .” he reached for his belt. “He’s *not* pulling over.”

Well, she had to agree with him. If he was the person responsible for all these murders, he had nothing to lose. He’d keep going until he was forced to stop. “Shoot the tires, then?”

Brisbane pulled out his gun. “Yeah. I don’t think I have any choice. Keep it steady,” he said, pointing his gun out the window, taking aim downward.

He pulled the trigger.

The first gunshot was followed by the ping of metal. The second, nothing. The car kept going. The third, Brisbane let out a “Shit,” and glared back at her. “*Steady.*”

“I am!” She really couldn’t possibly keep steadier. Was he that bad a shot?

The fourth shot hit its mark, because the truck suddenly veered off the road, headed for a barren oilfield, filled with pumpjacks, standing at even intervals like sentries. The pumps slowly moved, up and down, down and up, peaceful despite the appearance of the out-of-control truck, which finally skidded to a stop, about fifty yards from the interstate.

Rylie jammed on her brakes and made a slight U-turn, heading off after it.

“Where are you—” he started, but the answer quickly became obvious when she breached the edge of the interstate and headed out into the field, after the truck. “Oh.”

“This pick-up is made for off-roading,” she said, remembering the times Hal would take her in his truck, out on his vast ranch on the Wyoming-Montana border. She’d bought this pick-up, just because it’d reminded her of his. She loved the rough terrain underneath the wheels.

Brisbane, on the other hand, clutched at his stomach. “Easy.”

There was still some light in the sky by the time she reached the truck, though the sun had almost completely disappeared behind the mountain.

She braked hard, making out the suspect’s silhouette as he climbed out of the cab and tore off toward the pines in the distance.

Grabbing her gun, she took off in pursuit.

Brisbane did, too, but he wasn't as fast as she was. As she ran, the lights from the police car, parked up on the shoulder of the interstate, slashed across her vision. She ignored everything but her target, jumping over desert shrubs and rocks, throwing herself over narrow gullies, running around pumpjacks, giving chase. The man was in good shape, as well, but as he moved forward in the dying light, he must've second-guessed his footing, because he froze for a bit too long, trying navigate a ridge, and she managed to get close enough to stop and raise her gun.

"Stop right there! FBI!" she shouted.

The man froze, lifting his hands in the air before she even commanded him to do so. So at least he had some sense.

"Turn around."

He did, slowly. There was a smile on his face, like he was happy to be caught. "Hello," he said pleasantly. "Nice night for a stroll, huh?"

She recognized his face from the photograph she'd seen in his file. "Gary Vinton?"

He chuckled. "That's right. Seems my name precedes me. What's yours?"

"Where is Lila Garrity?" she demanded.

He lifted an eyebrow. "Who?"

"You heard me. Lila Garrity."

His chuckle became full laughter. "You think I know the names of all the women I become acquainted with? I'm sorry, darlin'. But I'm what you might call a ladies' man. I've got so many, they're crawling out of my ears. Can't keep none of them straight."

"Lila Garrity," she said, biting off each syllable. "And she didn't chase you. You're the one who ran her off the road before dragging her away from the crash site last night. Remember?"

Now, he simply looked amused. He mimed throwing a line and reeling it in. "Think you're fishing, darlin'. But I like it. I like your energy. It's sexy."

She couldn't take any more of this man's leering. "You're under arrest," she snarled with great satisfaction.

His grin widened. "I assumed so. But only if you get to pat me down, Agent . . ."

Her skin crawled. *I don't think so.*

Lyons and another officer appeared from behind her. She motioned to them, and they moved forward to snap the cuffs on him.

He tilted his head as they led him past her. "This isn't fair. You know all about me, and I know nothing about you." He laughed. "If I'd have known the FBI had such lookers, I'd have let myself get caught a long time ago."

Her instinct wanted her to rip that smug smile off his face. Instead, she looked away and motioned for them to get him out of her sight. She'd have to see him again, for questioning—she didn't want anyone else to handle that. But by then, she hoped she'd have her emotions under control.

She was still breathing hard, her heart pounding, when they put him in the police car. She turned and noticed him, in the window, his eyes still trained on her. "What a scumbag," she mumbled.

"We always knew that," Brisbane said, appearing beside her. Had he always been there? He held up a hand for a high-five. "Nice work, agent. We got our man."

She slapped his hand. "That, we did. I guess we need to talk to him and iron out the details, as soon as we can, so we can figure out what happened to Lila. She might be out there, somewhere."

Together, they started to walk back toward the interstate. They had a suspect to interview. As they reached Gary Vinton's black pick-up, she turned on her flashlight so she could study the front grill of the truck in the dying light. It was a nice truck, probably not cheap. Likely only a few years old.

And, as she observed with a sinking feeling, absolutely free of any dents, chips, or scratches.

Brisbane seemed to notice it at the same time she did, because he dragged his hand down his face and said, "Don't worry, Wolf. He's the one. I'm sure he is."

But she couldn't share his certainty. "I really hope you're right," she said quietly.

## CHAPTER TWELVE

Rylie sipped coffee and sighed as the police led the suspects into the line-up. It wasn't even seven o'clock, yet, and she was already exhausted.

Gary Vinton, number three, stood there, smirking. Facing life behind bars, and yet, he looked as happy as a clam. She wondered what on earth it would take to wipe that smile from his face.

Michael Brisbane sat at a desk with the girl who'd nearly been kidnapped. Petite and dainty, with a short pixie haircut, she looked much younger than her twenty-seven years, especially in her baggy, college-girl sweats and headband. Her name was Hazel Gray, and she hadn't stopped talking since she came into the station.

That was probably why she and Brisbane were getting on *famously*. It was amazing they were letting each other get a word in edgewise. Brisbane complimented her fingernails—since when did he care about manicures?—and she'd launched into a long, winding story about how she saw it on Instagram and she'd finally gotten one of the local shops to do it, just the way she'd wanted. She was so busy talking, waving her hands around in gestures bigger than her own body, that she didn't even notice when the suspects came in.

"Hazel," Rylie said, interrupting her story.

The girl stopped talking and looked at her.

"The suspects are lined up now. Now, keep in mind, this is one-way glass, so don't be afraid. You can see them, but they can't—"

"Number three," she said flatly, with utmost certainty.

Rylie stopped and glanced at the other officers in the room. They shrugged back. "Are you sure? You should take your time. Because—"

"No. I don't need to. That's the bastard right there. I'll never forget him. Such a creep. My car was making noises and I needed to get to Sheridan for my shift at the Y. When he showed up at the auto shop out of nowhere and offered me a ride, I thought he was an angel. Some angel." She smiled up at Brisbane. "So as I was saying . . ."

She went on talking, as one of the officers dipped his head to the intercom and instructed the officers in the room to take them out. Rylie finished her coffee and crunched up the paper cup. She looked at Brisbane, who was rapt. "Hey. Think we need to go interview—"

He blinked and seemed shocked to find Rylie standing there. Then he looked back at Hazel, and said, "Well . . . I think someone needs to interview the victim, right?"

She put her hands on her hips. "I don't think that's as pressing as speaking with the actual criminal. Do you?"

"Well, since there's two of us, maybe we can kill two birds at one time. Each tackle one of them?"

She stared at him, something strange boiling in her gut as they continued to converse about nothing that had to do with the attempted kidnapping. So he was going to "interview" the victim? Right. More like "get her number so he could ask her on a date."

"Missoula!" she blurted, patting her chest. "No, way! *I'm* from Missoula!"

"Seriously? That's awesome," he said, sounding every bit like a gawky teenager. "Grew up in North Dakota first years of my life, but Missoula's my home base."

Rylie had to exercise every bit of her own control to stop from stamping her foot like a tantrum-throwing toddler. "*Are* you going to interview her? Or are you just going to shoot the breeze all day?"

He reached into his pocket and pulled out a pad and pen. He waved her off, never looking at her.

That was it.

She let out a huff. "Fine!" she said, spinning on her heel and opening the door. "Whatever."

She'd been hoping that would make him realize it wasn't fine, and that he'd follow her. He didn't.

*Fine,* she thought. *Let him be so entranced by Miss Hazel Gray that he makes a damn fool of himself and undermines everything the FBI stands for.*

She took a few steps down the hall, muttering under her breath.

It shouldn't have bothered Rylie. After all, she called herself a Lone Wolf. In Seattle, she'd never lasted with a partner before, and she didn't want one. She thrived on handling everything herself.

But for some reason, as she heard Michael Brisbane erupt in genuine, unbridled laughter she'd never before heard from him, she felt a little sad. As if the entire world was moving on with their lives. And yet she never could. She'd always be that little girl, hiding in an RV, wondering, wondering, wondering what happened, until she was half-mad.

When she reached the door to the interrogation room, her gut twisted more.

So now she'd have to interview the creepy kidnapper guy who'd called her sexy, alone.

*Thanks, Bris.*

Taking a deep breath, she pushed open the door and went inside.

Lyons and another officer were already there, interviewing Vinton. They all stopped and looked up as she approached, sliding up against the wall. "Please. Continue. Don't let me bother you," she said.

Lyons said, "So why did you try to pick up that girl in Banner?"

He shrugged, never taking his eyes off Rylie. He licked his lips. "Told you this before. I wanted to have some fun."

"So you don't deny trying to pick her up today?"

He shook his head. "Does it look like I'm denying it?"

Rylie tried to keep quiet and let the police handle it. But she couldn't. When they looked at each other, unsure about what to ask, Rylie leaned forward. "What about Nina Maxwell?" she blurted.

He looked at her, his grin widening. "You throw around names like they're supposed to mean something to me. They don't."

"The girl you tried to pick up earlier this morning. Red hair, freckles?"

"Oh, yeah," he said, nodding. "I did pick her up. But I didn't do nothing wrong with her. I asked her if she wanted to have some fun, and she said she wouldn't. So I just dropped her off."

"Have you done anything wrong with *any* of the girls you picked up?" she demanded.

His smile faded.

*I'll take that as a yes,* Rylie thought. "Which ones?"

He pressed his lips together.

She placed her palms on the table and leaned in close. "We're going to find out, anyway. So trust me, it'll be much better for you if you just come clean."

He shook his head. "I didn't do nothin' wrong."

She crossed her arms. "You used to work as a truck driver for Swiftline Express, out of Missoula, a couple years ago. Did you go by the name of Vin, then?"

He nodded. "Everyone calls me Vin."

"When you were working for the trucking company, you were driving into Wyoming all the time, right?"

He nodded.

"You were friends with Clive McDougal. Were you not?"

He rubbed the stubble on his chin. "Yeah. I knew the guy. But what's this got to do with—"

"I have a sworn statement from Clive McDougal that you confessed to him that you kidnapped and murdered a girl. True?"

His eyes widened. "What?"

She stared at him, unblinking. "Is. It. True?"

He swallowed. "Look, I—"

"I have the case files for half a dozen women who were murdered on this stretch of I-86. All young and pretty, all alone, all—"

"Wait, no," he said, shaking his head fervently. "That ain't it. All right, all right. There was that one girl. She told me she was eighteen. I picked her up and we drove a little ways, and she told me she wanted me. And so . . . we pulled over and you know." He dragged both hands down his face. "But then she told me she was only fifteen. And I panicked. I knew I'd get in trouble if anyone found out. So . . . yeah. I slapped her. Maybe a little too hard. Just once, though."

"And?"

"And what?"

He shrugged. "I don't know. It was a long time ago."

"What was her name?" Rylie said quietly.

He shook his head. "I don't know. I only told Mac about it because we were drunk, and he was telling me about all these girls he got with. And I let it slip, and . . . *shit*." His smile was gone. His hands started to shake in his lap.

Rylie went through the files she'd brought in from her truck. She pulled out the photograph of Chrissy Johnson, the pretty fifteen-year-old who'd run away from home. "Was it her?"

He stared at the picture for a beat, then dropped his gaze and nodded. "Yeah. I'm sorry. I'm so sorry," he blubbered.

"You killed her? She died?"

He lowered his head. "Yeah. I guess. But it was an accident. I swear. That's all."

"What about Erin Littlefeather? Lisa Garrity? Did you run those girls off the road?"

He shook his head. "No. No, I swear. I didn't do anything to any of them. Look, I have a thing for picking up young hitchhikers on the road. I drive all over, looking for them. It's exciting to me, picking a girl up, having relations, dropping her off and never seeing her again. Sometimes I'm lucky, sometimes I ain't. But I didn't mean to kill anyone. You got to believe me."

"Where were you, yesterday afternoon?" she asked.

He thought. "Me? I was with my buddies. We were together at a bar called Hanson's, in Buffalo. Watching the rodeo on television. I was there all day, from about eleven to six at night. I know about a dozen people who saw me there."

She glanced at her feet. If that was true, and she had no reason to believe it wasn't, then it meant that he had an alibi for Erin Littlefeather's disappearance.

Was it possible there were two drivers of black trucks, terrorizing young girls in this area? "And last night?"

He shook his head. "Buddies again. You can ask any one of them. We play poker at my friend Ralph's house."

This didn't make any sense. She knew there was a lot of evil in the world, but this was too much . . .

When she looked up, Gary Vinton was smiling again. "Aw, I burst your bubble, didn't I? You thought you caught yourself a serial killer?" He let out a short burst of laughter. "Sorry to disappoint you. But you know what? I'm glad you found me. It's been on my conscience. I'm ready to confess and serve my time."

Rylie leaned into Lyons's ear and whispered, "See if you can pinpoint where he buried the girl."

Then she turned for the door and closed it behind her, letting out a sigh. So they'd solved one cold case—the disappearance of Chrissy Johnson. But Lila Garrity was still missing, and running out of time. And even more alarming, there was still another psycho out there.

And she had a feeling this one was worse.

As she reached the lobby, she saw Brisbane, saying goodbye to Hazel Gray. She smiled and waved at him, then turned and headed for the parking lot. He whirled, too, a goofy smile on his face.

Rylie rolled her eyes. "Done *questioning your subject?* If that's what you call it?"

He looked confused. "What's that supposed to mean?"

"Nothing," she muttered, wondering why she even cared. How he acted on the job had nothing to do with her. She stalked down the hallway and added, "Did you learn anything new?"

"Nah. He's clearly a creep. But I couldn't get much more from her. He didn't mention anything about the other girls to Hazel. You get anything from Vinton?"

She whirled to face him, a smile of satisfaction on her face. "Oh, nothing, really," she said in a lilting, nonchalant voice. "I just worked a confession for the Chrissy Johnson murder out of him."

His jaw dropped. "Seriously?"

She nodded. "Could've been you." *That'll teach you to put flirting over business.* She shrugged. "But instead, I get the gold star."

"Wow," he mouthed, shaking his head. "Just like that. Hell, did he say anything more about—"

"No. But we'll work on him," she said, grabbing her files and heading for the door. "The problem is that he couldn't have murdered Littlefeather. He has an alibi."

He stood there, watching her leave. "He couldn't have? Wait . . . where are you going?"

"Where do you think? We still have a killer on our hands. He has Lila Garrity. So I'm going to bring in all those case files and see if I can find any connections to past cold cases that might help us figure out who this guy is."

"Right," he said, following her. "Let's do this."

# CHAPTER THIRTEEN

An hour later, the little table in the break room was on the verge of collapse, under the weight of all the files they'd amassed. Rylie groaned as she read through another kidnapping case in Cheyenne—this one, committed by an old man in a red sportscar, clearly wasn't related. They'd even had Beeker run a check on anyone in the area with a criminal record and a black pick-up truck and send over those files. They were about halfway done with the files from the past ten years, but nothing seemed to stand out.

Brisbane closed a file, yawned, and stretched his arms over his head. "Find anything?"

She shook her head. "No. You?"

"Not a thing." He patted his stomach. "My stomach's growling."

She reached into her purse and pulled out a dollar. "Go get yourself something."

He made a face. "If I eat any more vending machine food, I'm going to be sick. What about steak? Lyons was going to get us take-out, remember? We could at least take a break and—"

"No. Not yet." An image of a scared Lisa Garrity, transposed on the face of her own sister, hovered in her mind. She blinked it away and pointed at the file. "I want to keep digging a little more."

"All right," he mumbled, taking the dollar from her and going to the vending machine. "One big stomachache, coming right up. But we *are* getting steak, later, tonight."

"Deal."

As he stood there, back to her, trying to decide which snack to get, she reached into the pile in front of her and pulled out a thick report that she hadn't seen. It was a kidnapping from decades ago, so probably not very useful in this case. She was about to place it on the rejects pile when her eyes caught on the name on the tab.

*Maren Wolf.*

She hesitated there, her palms growing slick with sweat as she stared at the file. It felt heavy, like a boulder in her hand. She slipped a finger underneath the file to open it, and took a deep breath, her body trembling. Then she lifted the cover and scanned the first line.

*Victim(s) Name(s): Maren Wolf, Nicole Wolf, Rose Green, Katherine Green.*

She stared at the names, right there, in black and white. Her entire childhood, wrapped up in a single line. All of them, gone.

Her hands shook as she turned the page to see a smiling school photograph of Maren. She'd been twelve at the time, and the photograph was her sixth-grade school photo. She'd been skinny, all angles, and hadn't reached puberty yet, so she was still very much a little girl, her hair in two long braids behind her ears.

The photograph of her mom was one with all of them, the whole family. Nicole Wolf had been sitting in a lounge chair, on the curb, for a town parade, waving a tiny American flag. She was wearing a sleeveless shirt, tied at the belly, platform sandals and short shorts, her long, tanned legs crossed. Maren and Rylie flanked her, their arms around her. She was wearing sunglasses, so it was impossible to see her pretty eyes, and her dark hair was blown slightly into her face.

Was that the only photo they had of her? Didn't her dad have anything better? Maybe not. Nicole Wolf dreaded the spotlight.

She flipped past the other photos, the crimes scene photos, her stomach roiling, her throat closing. She couldn't breathe. She tried to gasp for air but it felt like it had all been sucked from the room. She coughed, her face heating, and—

*Snap.*

She blinked, tearing her eyes away from the page, and looked up at Brisbane, who was chewing on a chip from a Doritos bag. "Hey. You all right?"

Her eyes fell to the papers in front of her. No, she was most certainly not all right, after what had happened to her.

But it was the last thing she wanted him to know about.

She squeezed the papers against her chest. "No, I mean . . . I'm fine," she said, closing the file and burying it deep underneath the others. "It's just—seeing all these horrible crimes sometimes gets to me. You know how it is?"

He nodded. "Sure do. It's hard."

Though by the nonchalant way he popped a chip into his mouth, one wouldn't know it.

*Nice save,* she thought, reaching for another file from the top of the pile.

"But . . ." he said, sitting down beside her. His eyes were narrowed in concern. "I got to admit, you looked a little spooked just then. Are you sure everything's all right? Did you see something in one of the files?"

She stiffened. "What?"

"Like . . . that file. You looked like—I don't know—for a second, I thought you were going to . . . cry."

*Cry?* Probably. But that was the last thing she ever wanted to do on the job. The thing she swore she'd never do again, after that day.

She averted her eyes. "Bris . . . I don't know what you're talking about."

"Just—"

"Oh, my God," she said loudly, clapping a file closed and throwing it down on the table. "I just told you I was fine! So stop beating a dead horse and drop it, all right?"

He just stared at her, long enough for her to feel guilty for losing her cool and snapping at him like that. Then he shrugged and said, quietly, "All right," and reached for the next folder.

"Look," she said after a few silent, tense moments. "I don't mean to be a jerk but a girl is out there, she needs our help, and we have to get through these files as fast as possible. That's all."

He didn't look up. "Yeah. Got it."

For once, he wasn't his chatty self, and almost instantly, she missed that about him.

Still, that was it. She'd silenced his questions, for now.

But it wasn't the end. She knew that much. Until she had answers as to who had kidnapped Maren and killed the people she loved, it would never be the end.

# CHAPTER FOURTEEN

It was time, now.

Now that the sun had gone down and he'd gotten far enough away from civilization, he could take his time. One wonderful thing about this state was that there were plenty of remote locations for this kind of thing. He'd driven onto the property of an old, unused coal mine, surrounded by buttes. In the desolation, a coyote howled. Stars overhead twinkled, as if to say he'd done a good job.

Yes, this would work perfectly.

His permanent smile widened as he pulled himself out from behind the wheel of his truck. His boots hit the dusty ground, and he stepped toward the back of his truck, unlocking the tailgate. Then he pulled open the cover and shined a flashlight into the dark space.

The girl was there, awake and alert as ever, eyes wide. She trembled and shrunk away from him as he reached for her.

"Now, don't be shy," he said, moving closer, hands out. "I was shy, once, too, but I learned that shyness is not the way to go."

He grabbed her and slid her closer to him on the tailgate. Her wrists and ankles were bound together, and he'd placed duct tape over her mouth. He looked down at her, admiring her beauty, a beauty that he would never possess himself.

Then he pried up the corner of the tape with his fingernail and ripped it off, roughly.

It probably hurt, considering the red, raw skin that was left behind, a bloody rectangle. The second the tape was free, she started to scream.

That was all right. He liked it. It was like fighting, clawing. He enjoyed the reaction.

But it was completely for naught.

She could scream as loud as she wanted, here. No one would ever hear her.

He watched her, trying to be patient, but his hands shook in his excitement. "Are you done yet?" She continued to scream. "How about now?"

Clearly not. She screamed and screamed until she started to choke. Then, as she was gasping for breath, she said, "Please. Please don't do this."

A low laugh erupted from his chest.

He'd thought the same thing, seventeen years ago, while he'd sat in the front seat of his father's pick-up truck. *Don't do this.*

But some things had to happen. His father had been right. The girl had been in the wrong. She'd caused this. Caused him a lifetime of pain and self-loathing.

With that thought in his head, he pulled the gloves from the pocket of his barn jacket. He separated them, then snapped one of them on each of his hands.

Then he slipped his hands around the blonde's neck, making sure her eyes were on his.

They widened to full moons as the realization crept in. This was it. He loved that moment. The moment they realized there was nothing left they could do. It was too late.

He lifted her gently, and then he began to squeeze, feeling the ridges of her windpipe, buckling, gasping. He squeezed so hard that the tongue popped out of her mouth like a jack-in-the-box, and he heard the unmistakable snap of a bone.

And then she was gone. Too quickly, too easily, almost. He'd thought she was scrappier than that. That she'd last longer.

Disappointment crowded his features, though his smile remained intact as always. Gone too soon. Damn.

Part of it was his own fault. He should've taken more time. Like with that Lakota girl. That had been lovely. He'd squeezed just enough for her to feel it, then he'd laid off, then he'd squeezed again, slightly harder each time, until he'd built to that glorious climax.

But he'd been too excited, this time. He'd put it off too long, and so he'd been shaky and nervous and the anticipation had been too great.

One thing was certain, though.

He needed more.

He shoved her lifeless body into the back of the truck and locked the tailgate. Then he went to the front of his car and pulled open the door.

As usual, almost the instant he gripped the handle, he broke out in a cold sweat.

His mind cycled through distorted images. Headlights flashing across his face. The sound of a horn, blaring in his ears. The branches of that pine tree, rushing up to meet him, and him, able to do nothing but close his eyes and wait for impact.

The impact, he didn't remember.

What he did remember were years and years of physical therapy. Surgery after surgery, all ending with a surgeon shaking his head and uttering some version of, *Well, we did the best we could, but the damage was just too extensive.* The community had rallied around him, at first. But then they got their first look at him. And they did not want another. The *Get Well Soon* cards stopped coming. Then, the taunts started.

After that, he resigned himself to a dark room in his house. For years. Not just because the pain of their rejection had been worse than any surgery he'd had. No, it was also because he couldn't bear to look at the inside of a truck again.

Eventually, though, he'd forced himself.

He'd said that if he was ever going to make amends for what happened, he couldn't do it from under his bed.

Now, he was stronger than ever.

Once he got in, it wasn't a big deal. But it was simply choosing to do so that was the hard thing. His mind lingered on the question . . .*Should I? Shouldn't I?* and his throat started to constrict.

His fear of vehicles was very much like his fear of the outside. He had to face it.

And once he did, things always got better. One he started up the engine, he felt invincible. Immortal.

Tightening his hands into fists, he took a deep breath and let it out. Then he slipped into the seat. Before closing the door, he did what he always did.

He lit a cigarette.

He took a few puffs, letting the smoke surge through his lungs, calming him. When he puffed out, he already felt better.

More in control.

The ruler of this domain.

He started the engine, and he smiled up at the night sky. There was a yearning in him that would not be quenched tonight. Not with that weak girl.

He needed another one.

The Scarred Man pulled onto the road, heading toward the interstate. When it was in view, the taillights of the few cars on it visible as just pinpoints in the night, he realized he'd have to finish one job in order to start another.

He pulled to the side of the road and dumped the body in a line of desert bushes. Unceremonious, yes, but her death had been ordinary. Probably just like her life had been. It was fitting.

Then, he got into the car, hands shaking until he lit up another cigarette. Relaxing, he licked his lips at the thought of what was to come.

This time, he'd take his time. He'd find a new one fast, but once he had her, he'd go nice and slow. He wouldn't gorge himself like a starving man at a great feast. No, he'd observe it all, with every one of his senses. And he'd let himself experience every last gasp, every last whimper, every touch. He'd drink it in, and love it all.

Because he was the master, here.

And no one would forget.

# CHAPTER FIFTEEN

Rylie continued to piece through the files, finding nothing of interest.

It was getting later and later, and soon they'd probably have to find a hotel to stay for the night. They hadn't had dinner, either, which Brisbane was probably sour about, though he'd walked away, shortly after she'd exploded on him.

Why had she done that?

She'd been feeling guiltier and guiltier about the outburst, snapping at him. She'd wanted to stay professional. But he needed to understand. She was able to withstand most of his bad habits, but she couldn't deal with him poking into her private life. That was absolutely where she drew the line.

Still, he didn't know that. She needed to make it clear to him, the next time she spoke to him.

*No, not next time,* she told herself. *You have more important things on your mind to deal with right now.*

She forced the thoughts out of her head and tried to bury her nose in the files. As she did, a larger figure came in. She thought it was Brisbane, but it was Officer Lyons. "Making any progress?"

"Not really," she said as he poured himself a cup of coffee. "Did you get anything more from Gary Vinton about where he buried Chrissy Johnson's body?"

He nodded. "Yep. We got a good idea. It's an old mine north of Sheridan. But Chief says we should wait until first light to check it out. Otherwise it's a wild goose chase, not to mention the danger of falling down a shaft."

She didn't need to be told that one. She'd been thrown down a mine during the last case, by an insane murderer, and her back still hurt whenever she thought about it. "Gotcha. Where is Agent Brisbane?"

"Oh." He motioned toward the door. "He's at an empty desk out there, digging through some of your files."

She blinked. "Really? Why?"

"Well . . . he said he thought you needed some time alone."

*Which is the polite, Michael Brisbane way of saying he didn't want to be near me.*

She grimaced. "What does that mean? I didn't tell him that! I'm fine," she mumbled, but she understood it. No one probably wanted to be in the company of her, the unleashed Kraken.

Lyons stood there, shifting from foot to foot. "Well . . ."

"Forget it." She glanced down at the folder in front of her, as something occurred to her.

"Get him back in here. I have something to say."

He leaned back, poking his head out the door. "Uh . . . actually, I don't really know if he wants to talk to you."

She almost laughed out loud. "Well, we're partners, so he has to. Bris!" she shouted. "Get in here."

A few moments later, he appeared in the doorway. "You called."

That trademark smile was gone. Was he really still sore about her snapping at him?

She'd have to apologize. But right now, they had work to do.

"It just occurred to me. He's taking these pretty young girls and holding them for a time. He must want them for something. Right?"

Brisbane shrugged. "Yeah. But what?"

"I don't know. The obvious answer is for something sexual. Just like Gary Vinton. Right?"

Brisbane shook his head. "Erin Littlefeather's autopsy didn't reveal any sexual assault. The medical examiner said that it didn't look like her clothes had been removed at any time."

She frowned. "I don't remember hearing that."

"I think it was during one of your zone-out moments," he mumbled.

Zone-out moments? Great, so she was spacing out. Exploding on him. Acting oddly. No wonder he didn't want to be in the same room as her. "All right. But maybe that's what he wanted, but they refused to give it up."

His eyes narrowed. "You mean that they declined his advances, and so he killed them?"

She nodded.

"I don't think so. Maybe. But not likely. If he was able to overpower her to kill her, then he was in the position to take what he wanted in the first place. Why didn't he didn't he sexually assault her then?"

Rylie sighed. He was absolutely right. If that was the killer's aim, then it would've shown on the autopsy. "That means that the killer wanted to keep her for some other reason. What?"

He shook his head.

She looked at the file of another young girl. She'd been raped and murdered, a couple years ago, around the Sheridan area. "Maybe he just wants to toy with them," she mumbled, mostly to herself. That was the thing about getting into the mind of a killer—sometimes their actions defied logic.

And if they defied logic, maybe all of this profiling they were doing wouldn't amount to anything.

"We should still probably round up a list of sexual predators in the area," Rylie said, glancing at Lyons. "You think you can help with that?"

Officer Lyons sprang to attention. "Absolutely, Agent. I was actually just updating one of those today, on account of the fact that our biggest one was just released from prison two days ago."

She and Brisbane exchanged glances. "The biggest sexual predator in the area was just released from prison two days ago?" she asked.

Officer Lyons nodded slowly, then it was like a lightning bolt hit him, out of nowhere. "Wait . . . do you think . . .?"

They nodded in unison. "Can you get us an arrest report on him?" Brisbane prompted.

"His name's Bennett Hoscomb," Lyons said with a nod. "We all know him around here. He's been in and out of jail forever. I always thought there was something pretty creepy about him. The way he used to go to bars and—"

"Get us that report, and we'll take it from here," she said impatiently, catching Brisbane glaring at her. She added, "Please."

He ran off, leaving them alone. Rylie laced her fingers in front of her. "About what I said to you before . . ."

He shrugged. "No big deal. We all go through shit."

"I wasn't going through any—" She stopped.

It was her constant denial that had gotten her snapping at him in the first place. If she'd just opened up to him and told him she had a family tragedy, maybe he wouldn't have pried. Maybe he would've just left it at that.

No wonder she'd never had a partner for long. Having a partner involved trust. Depending. Understanding. She never offered that to him, didn't want him to offer the same to her. He had every right to want to keep his distance.

She was about to open her mouth to apologize when Lyons appeared with the report. He held it out and cleared his throat. "So listen to this. Bennett L Hoscomb has been charged with assault and battery, sexual assault, theft, public nuisance . . . just about everything. Most recently, he was in for sexual abuse of a minor." He shook his head. "Yeah, ol' Ben's a real piece of w—"

Rylie grabbed the report and scanned down a long list of offenses. "This looks interesting," she said, offering it to Brisbane to look at. When he nodded, she flipped the page to find a photograph of a man in a cowboy hat, mid-fifties, with a long, curly gray beard and round, tinted spectacles. She looked for an address, but didn't find one. "It says 'no known abode.'"

Lyons nodded. "Yeah, he has a lot of girlfriends. Bounces around among them all."

Great. That didn't narrow things down much. This area of the country might have been sparsely populated, but combing all of Sheridan and its outlying areas was like looking for one particular needle among a pile of needles. "You have any idea where he works? Or who he might be staying with, so we can check him out?"

He shook his head, but then his eyes lit up. "Wait. I don't know where he's living, but every night about this time, he's at Willy's."

"What is Willy's?"

"It's a dive bar in Sheridan. He practically has his own stool dedicated to him, there. He's usually drunk. And--" He suddenly froze, as if he'd seen a ghost.

"And?"

A smile broke out on his face. "And I know for a fact that he drives a beaten-up black pick-up."

Rylie smiled and slammed her hands on the table.

"Well, that's it. Perfect." She stood up and grabbed her jacket and bag. "Then I think we should go and have a talk with him. What do you say, Bris?"

Brisbane clapped his hands and smiled. As he did, she could've sworn she heard his stomach rumble. "All right. My favorite thing is talking to drunk scumbags in dive bars at dinnertime. Lead the way."

# CHAPTER SIXTEEN

Michael Brisbane clamped a hand over his growling stomach.

What could he say? He'd done his usual five-mile run that morning, in the basement gym of the apartment he was renting in Rapid City, and after that, he'd had a banana. Then some pistachios, and a Snickers. After that, some Doritos, all washed down by copious amounts of coffee.

It would've been nice to have something *real* to eat.

But though he'd only been on the beat with Rylie Wolf for a couple weeks, he already knew that food was always the last thing on her mind. As was pretty much everything else except the case at hand. She had tunnel vision when it came to chasing answers. Nothing else mattered.

Which was probably why, every time he tried to socialize with her, find out a little more about her past, she shut him down.

The woman was a closed book.

As he sat in the front passenger seat of her truck, he looked around, trying to gauge what he could about her. So far, all he'd learned was that she came from Seattle, worked for the BAU there, and that she really didn't like sharing.

She also didn't like *eating* either, apparently. She didn't like a lot of things.

Including, he had the feeling, *him*.

That was something that completely baffled him. He hadn't had the easiest of lives. He'd had to scratch and claw his way into the FBI, like most agents. But despite his hardships, there was one thing that he always had going for him—his affable personality. People just liked him. He could talk to anyone, get even the grumpiest person to open up.

But Rylie? So far, no dice.

And he needed it. He wasn't used to being partners with a closed book. It was probably his own feelings of abandonment, but he craved some kind of connection. Some kind of trust. When people didn't talk, when they kept secrets. . . that bred misunderstanding. Distrust. It wasn't good.

As they drove toward Willy's Bar, he decided to try again. It was a tactic he'd employed to success a number of times. Basically, he just talked about himself until the other person felt compelled to share, too. He'd done it before, and yet so far, it only seemed to annoy Rylie. But a couple hours ago, he'd gotten the sense she felt guilty for snapping at him. Maybe he'd caught her with her walls down. So he'd give it one last shot.

"Yeah, so I've heard of this Willy's. It's a real honky-tonk. You ever been to one of those?"

She glanced at him. "Nope."

"Really? I lived down in Texas for a year. Right out of school. One on every corner, there. Used to be, you didn't like country music, they'd run you out of town. Not so much anymore," he said, drumming his fingers on the armrest. "You like it?"

He couldn't be sure she was even listening. After a long beat, she said, "What?"

"Country music. You like it?"

She motioned to the radio. "If you want to turn something on, go ahead."

Of course, she wasn't going to make it easy. But if he turned on the radio, he'd at least know what station she had it set to, and that would tell him *something* about her.

*Rylie Wolf, I am going to figure you out yet,* he thought, switching it on.

There was nothing but static.

Typical.

He turned it off. "So . . .," he said, not really sure where he was headed. "You miss Seattle?" When she didn't answer, he added, "I grew up in a town called Minot, North Dakota. First years of my life. You know it?"

"Hmm."

"Anyway, it's called the Magic City, which makes it sound like there are leprechauns and fairies in meadows there. But I couldn't really say it was all that magical. It was cold. I was kind of happy when my family moved to Missoula. Not that Missoula's not cold, but hell, it was different . . ."

He'd begun to think about his parents, and realized he was running his mouth. Sometimes he'd just do that—talk and talk, verbalizing his thoughts without realizing it.

But Rylie, clearly, had the opposite problem.

He said, "It's probably a lot colder here than in Seattle. Bet it was hard to get used to."

By then, he'd expected she wouldn't answer him. He was about to talk about his grandfather who fell in a mine shaft when he was twenty-six and froze to death, when she said, almost so quietly she couldn't be heard, "I'm actually from Wyoming."

He blinked. She was?

That was the first thing she'd ever willingly shared about herself. Well, he'd pried it out. But for a moment, he just stared at her, not knowing what to do with this new information. She was from here. "You move out when you were young?"

"Younger. I moved to Seattle for college."

So she'd lived here her entire young life. And yet if it'd had some impression on her, he never would've known. Except . . . what was the deal with the file she'd been studying? He'd gotten a look at it. Something about a triple-murder. She'd shoved it in with all the other files before he could see more.

Did she have something to do with that?

Maybe. Maybe not. But one thing was obvious. There were things she wanted to keep close to her chest. Still, he was an expert at dragging things out of people. And he'd do it. If it killed him, if *she* killed him, he would.

"So what made you move all the way to Sea—"

"There it is," she said, slowing to a stop at a large log-framed building with a neon sign above the doors. *Willy's Honky-Tonk—Best Country in the USA!*

The place looked like a pick-up truck dealership. The huge gravel lot was so full of them that the only parking was on the grass. There were also a number of Harleys parked in front. A couple of rough looking guys in cowboy hats and leather were smoking outside.

If Rylie was worried about her first time in one of these places, one wouldn't have known. She hopped out as soon as she parked and jogged to the front, so fast that he had to skip into a run to keep up.

"Someone means business," he said, rushing ahead to grab the door for her. As he did, he glanced back at the two men, smoking outside. They were eying them curiously.

"Always," she said.

The place was a wall of heat and smoke, despite the NO SMOKING signs posted everywhere. The smell, a curious combination of whisky, leather, cigarettes, and cooked beef, only made Michael's stomach rumble more. Appropriately, George Straight's "Every Little Honky Tonk Bar" was playing.

The moment the doors closed behind them, every eye went to them.

He leaned over to Rylie's ear. "We look like FBI agents."

She shrugged. "So? We *are* FBI agents."

"I don't think they really like Feds around here," he said, looking around uncomfortably.

"Hmm. I don't really care *what* they like," she said, brazenly stepping forward and working her way through the packed crowd toward the bar.

Michael filed in behind her, glancing around at all the men with their beards and cowboy hats. They approached the bar, but the bartender was on the other end of it, handing out beers to customers.

There was one open barstool there. He motioned for Rylie to take it, but when she refused, he slid onto it himself and drummed his hands on the sticky tile surface of the bar.

A woman at the seat next to him, with straight blonde hair and a short denim skirt and cowboy boots turned around and smiled. "You look like you took a wrong turn, darlin'."

"We're looking for Bennett Hoscomb," he said to her. "Do you know him?"

Her smile fell. She looked around at the other huge men that surrounded her. They all seemed to look into their beers, like there was something they didn't want to say. "What do you want him for?"

"Questioning," Rylie said, joining him. Michael had been reluctant to show his badge among this crowd, but she had no such fear. She flipped her credentials, business-like. "Is he here?"

The blonde looked around. "No. You just missed him, I think. Lucky for you."

"We need to talk to him. It's in your best interest to help us out," Rylie said, in that flat, demanding tone of hers. He had to hand it to her—she was tough. But she had absolutely no filter, and either didn't seem to realize, or didn't seem to care, when she was rubbing people the wrong way.

Predictably, the woman glared at her, a little taken aback. "Listen, honey . . . you can't come in here with that badge of yours and--"

Michael spoke quickly, trying to defuse any growing tensions.

"So he *was* here?" he asked, scanning the faces of the men around them, looking for the bearded man in the photograph. There were quite a few to choose from, but none of them looked quite right.

The smile reappeared. "Few minutes ago, darlin'. I don't know how long." She let out a long whistle that managed to quiet the crowd. "Anyone see where ol' Ben went?"

The men around her looked anywhere but at her, avoiding eye contact.

She shrugged at Michael. "Sorry, darlin', but he is and he ain't real popular around here, if you know what I mean. If you're on his good side, he'll treat you like a king, but if you're on his bad side, he'll tear you to pieces. Problems is, from day to day, you never know which you are. So most people like to steer clear of him."

"So he's a pretty nasty piece of work, huh?" Michael said with a charming smile as the bartender approached. He motioned to Rylie, himself, and the blonde, lifted three fingers, and mouthed, *We'll have three of whatever she's having.*

"Why, thank you, honey!" she said as the bartender placed three mugs of light amber beer on the bar. She took a sip. "Yes, he's one you don't want to cross. Though I'm sure you'll find out soon."

He leaned in and tried to take a sip of his beer, but got mostly foam. He felt it bubbling on his top lip. "Why's that?"

She leaned in. "He's been known to rip a guy a new one just for sitting in his stool," she said. "And you're in it."

Michael nearly choked on his mouthful of beer. He managed to swallow and slip off the stool at the same time.

Rylie snorted at him. She pushed the beer away, slipped onto the stool, and glaring around in a challenging way, said, "Do you have any idea where he might be?"

The woman shrugged. "I don't know. Could've just gone out for a cigarette. Or maybe he found a lady friend? Ben's not an airport. He ain't really fond of announcing his departure."

Michael looked at Rylie, who seemed to be getting more and more annoyed by the people around her, drinking and dancing. talking too loud. They were having fun, something Michael wondered if she'd ever done herself. Someone elbowed her in the ribs by accident and she scowled. "Do you mind?" she muttered, nudging them away. She motioned to Michael. "This is a waste of time. Let's get out of here."

Once again, he found himself behind her as she forged a trail through the bodies. When they were outside on the porch, a cold wind whipped through her hair. She smoothed it down and scanned the parking lot, huffing in frustration.

"Hey. You know, it's pretty late," Michael suggested as a couple of drunk girls came stumbling out of the bar, giggling.

One of the girls nearly slipped down the front stairs. He reached over to steady her right in time. She burst out laughing and said, "My hero!" She patted his chest. "Cutie in a *suitie*."

Rylie cleared her throat. "Hello?"

He smiled at the girls as they rushed off, then turned to face Rylie, who was scowling at him. What, was he supposed to let the girl fall? "Yeah . . . as I was saying, it's pretty late. Maybe we should just call it a night and find a—"

"Bris. Look."

He followed her line of sight to the edge of the road. The two drunken girls had tottered over there in their short skirts and cowboy boots, and were now standing under a streetlight, shivering and hugging their bare arms in the cold.

A man with a beard and a cowboy hat was standing with them.

As they watched, he reached into the back pocket of his jeans, pulled out his wallet, and fished some money out, offering it to them. From where they stood, they could hear the girls' giggles across the parking lot.

"Is that what—and who—I think it is?" Rylie asked.

"Pretty damn close. You saw his picture." He squinted, trying to get a look of the man, who, in profile, looked very much like the photograph he'd seen. "Kind of looks like him, doesn't it?"

"Yeah, I'd say," she said, stepping forward. "And he's propositioning those girls for sex."

The girls started to walk away from him. "It looks like whatever he's buying, they're not selling." He rubbed his finger and thumb over his rough five o'clock shadow, half-formed ideas for their next steps cycling in his head. They could probably follow his truck to wherever he was headed, if they waited. "So what do you think we should—"

"Hoscomb!" she shouted across the lot.

He turned around and looked at them, then bolted for the edge of the road. Before he could even register what was happening, she tore off after him.

Well, that was one thing they could do. Not his first choice, but . . . *fine*.

With no other options, he took off in pursuit. He might have been a runner, but he'd never run on such an empty stomach. He had a stitch in his side, the moment he reached the trees at the edge of the lot.

By the time he broke past the trees, both Rylie and Hoscomb were gone.

Breathing hard, he looked around, trying to figure out where they went. Then he cupped his hands around his mouth and shouted, "Wolf!"

But no one answered back.

He jogged forward, not sure where he was headed. Rylie was chasing after a dangerous sexual criminal, and she was nowhere to be found. This wasn't good.

He had to find her.

# CHAPTER SEVENTEEN

Rylie raced into the cold night, against the cold wind.

As she ran, pumping her legs and arms as fast as she could, his moving form on the side of the road seemed to get smaller and smaller. He was getting away. His cowboy hat blew off his head, disappearing into the darkness, but he didn't hesitate. God, he was fast.

Soon, she couldn't see him at all.

She kept running, even though he was no longer in her sight, hoping her eyes were playing tricks on her. But after a few seconds, she realized she was chasing air.

She was just about to slow when a form jumped out from the roadside drainage ditch, grabbing both of her legs. It all happened so fast that, before she could put out her hands to break her fall, she found herself horizontal on the rough gravel, its sharp edges digging into the exposed skin of her cheeks and hands.

He pulled her into the gulley, and she was helpless to stop it. The world spun upside down until her head came crashing to the hard earth. She looked up and saw two eyes gazing at her, narrowed into slits. "Who the hell are you?" he sneered, spittle spraying her face.

She tried to move out from underneath his thick body, but he held her wrists tight above her head. His knee was jammed against her chest, threatening to crush it. Somehow, though, she managed the question she wanted him to answer.

"Rylie Wolf. FBI. Did you kill those girls?"

His eyes widened slightly. He reached down under her jacket, groping her until her found her ID. He pulled it out and looked at the badge, glinting in the moonlight. "Hell."

"Let me go."

He shook his head. "No. You need to understand. I didn't kill no one. They're not gonna pin nothing on me. I just got out of prison a couple days ago."

"The two girls disappeared within the past two days."

He was still shaking his head. "Well, it ain't me. I didn't do anything—"

"FBI! Freeze! Hands up and turn around!" Michael Brisbane's voice called, firm and authoritative, against the wind.

Bennett Hoscomb froze, but he took his time loosening his grip on her. Then, he pushed off her and stood, raising his hands.

She sat up and breathed a sigh of relief. "Where were you?"

"I lost you. Didn't expect we'd be going on a sprint," he said, grabbing Hoscomb by the collar and patting him down. "Call the police and get them here. Let's bring this guy in for questioning."

She grabbed her phone from her pocket and started to make the call when, suddenly, their suspect wrenched his way out of Brisbane's grip, elbowing him in the chest and taking off like a bolt of lightning.

"Shit!" Brisbane said, reaching for him, then for his gun, but it was too late. The guy tore off through the trees, headed back toward Willy's.

"He's probably going for his vehicle!" Rylie shouted, taking off again. After her fall, she was beaten and bruised, a bit dizzy, and a little slower on the uptake. But she gained her momentum back as she continued to run. She got back to the parking lot in time to see headlights of a pick-up truck, pulling out of its parking space. "Oh, no you don't!"

She lunged forward and grabbed the passenger-side door, just as Hoscomb was shifting into drive. It was only as she was pulling open the door and climbing inside the cab that she realized something.

It was a dark-colored, navy-blue pick-up truck with tinted windows.

This was looking better and better, by the second. She didn't care if he decided to throw her out of the moving truck. She'd hold on. She could *not* let this guy get away.

"What part about 'FBI! Freeze!' don't you understand?" she shouted at him, reaching for her gun.

"What the hell are you—crazy bitch!" He jammed on the brakes and tried to shove her out of the half-opened door.

But she managed to wrangle her gun free of its holster and point it at him.

"I wouldn't. And if you try that again, you're going to have a bullet in your head." She motioned to the dashboard. "Cut the engine."

Scowling, he reached over and turned the key. The truck stopped its idle. Then he stared straight ahead and jammed his hands on the steering wheel, hard.

"Dammit!" he shouted, shaking his head. "I don't know what you're thinking you're going to get from me."

“The truth. That’s all,” she said, feeling rather good about this. After all, he’d tried to run away. You didn’t do that if you were innocent.

“You people. You stupid people. Always pinning things on me. Won’t ever leave me alone.”

“Maybe you should try to keep your nose clean and stay out of trouble?” she suggested, holding her gun at the steady as Brisbane appeared in view.

She powered down the window as Hoscomb said, “I was! I was just at the bar, having a good time.”

“You have two FBI agents who witnessed you trying to solicit sex from those girls. You’ve been arrested before for it, so you should know that it’s illegal.”

He sunk lower in his seat, defeated.

Brisbane came to a stop behind her, breathing hard. He said, “Damn, you’re fast. How did you—”

“Dark pick-up,” she said with a triumphant smile.

“I see that. And I think you got guts, girl. Did you know you were this close to being a smear on the pave--”

She waved him off. “Just call the cops so we can bring this guy in and find out what he knows.”

# CHAPTER EIGHTEEN

By the time they made it back to the police station, it was after ten at night. Rylie trudged in, fighting the urge to yawn.

She needed to stay awake and alert for this questioning. Bennett Hoscomb was a career criminal and had already proven he'd do whatever it took to evade them. He was comfortable around law enforcement—too comfortable. That meant that he could lie easily, without giving himself away.

She went to pour herself her ninth cup of coffee that day, and found Michael Brisbane in the break room, already getting her a cup. He handed it to her. "How're you feeling?"

How many times was he going to ask her if she was all right? "What do you mean? Like I said--"

He pointed to her forehead. "You have a bruise. Do you need to get that looked at?"

She touched it. Sure enough, it was tender. She looked around for some reflective surface but only found the window. It wasn't the best reflection, but even so, she could see an angry purple bruise sprouting, just above her temple. Lovely. "It's fine. I didn't even know I had it."

"That was some kind of Captain America stuff you performed. Jumping into a moving vehicle?" He raised both eyebrows.

She couldn't tell if he was impressed, or if he thought she was insane.

"It wasn't really moving." She headed for the interrogation room, but stopped. "But thank you for coming to my rescue, there."

"Hey. If I'd been a faster runner, it wouldn't have happened in the first place."

She shrugged and put her hand on the doorknob to the room. "Look. Can you—"

"Let you take the lead with questioning?" He leaned against the wall and smirked. "Sure."

She blinked, surprised. "How did you know I was going to—"

"Because you always want to take the lead. With everything," he said with a shrug, taking a sip of his coffee. "Only this time, I'm all for it. I'm beat. I'm only firing on a few brain cells right now."

She held up the coffee. "Don't worry. I've got this."

Steeling her expression, she pushed open the door. Officer Lyons was standing in the corner, and Bennett Hoscomb was seated at the table in the center of the bare room, wrists cuffed in front of him, shoulders slumped. He simply looked guilty, because he was.

But was he guilty of murder? That was the question.

As she sat down across from him, he smiled. "That's an awful bruise, agent."

She exhaled slowly. "I didn't introduce myself before. I'm Rylie Wolf of the FBI, and this is my associate, Michael Brisbane. Don't feel you need to introduce yourself, because, Mr. Hoscomb, we already know quite a bit about you. It's all on your rap sheet."

He shrugged. "So?"

"So . . . what have you been doing since you got out of prison?"

"Little of this. Little of that. I only got out a couple days ago. Mostly just meeting with old friends, trying to pull things back together again. Been working, too."

She glanced down at his folder. "Says here that you mostly do odd jobs around town. Is that right?"

"Yeah. Turns out, not many places will hire an ex-con. So I get money where I can. I'm handy. I did a couple jobs on a friend's ranch."

"And where were you this morning, at around ten o'clock?"

"On the ranch. Fixing a fence."

"You were? Anyone able to vouch for you?"

He shook his head. "My friend doesn't hold my hand. He was at an auction, which is why he needed someone else to do it. So I guess I'm SOL, huh?"

He didn't seem terribly bothered by that. In fact, he seemed happy to be able to meddle in their investigations. Rylie couldn't help getting the feeling that everything he was saying was a taunt, a half-truth. Like all of this was a game to him. "What about last night, at around midnight?"

"Ah. Now that, I can help you with. I was with a girl. Gertrude Blinkens. All night."

Rylie's spirits plummeted. He had an alibi?

Officer Lyons leaned in. "Gertie Blinkens is a well-known prostitute around here. She's been in jail more than she's out."

Hoscomb looked up at him and scowled. "You can't prove I paid her."

Lyons scoffed. "Yeah? I bet we could bring her in here and offer her immunity, and she'd tell us exactly what happened. She isn't loyal to any of her johns."

Rylie didn't care about that. All she cared about was that if he was with this Gertie woman, he couldn't have kidnapped Lila Garrity. And that meant . . .

Back to the drawing board.

No. Maybe he was lying. She had a find a way to make sure his alibi was airtight. And that meant, poking holes and seeing if anything leaked.

He shrugged. "If she tells you I paid her, then she's a damn liar." His eyes fell on Rylie. "But the fact remains, I was with her."

"From what time?"

"Eight at night . . . to probably about seven in the morning."

"You stay in a hotel?"

"Yep."

"Which one?"

He grinned and said, "The Mountain Super 8 in Buffalo," he said, and motioned down with his chin. "If you want to reach in my back pocket and get my wallet, I can show you the receipt. I bet it even has check-in and check-out times."

She looked a Brisbane. He said, "You could've gone somewhere in between."

"But I didn't."

"And Gertie will vouch for that?" Rylie asked.

He shrugged. "I don't know what she'll say. Can't trust no woman. But the place has cameras, and they don't lie."

Lyons scoffed. "Just like it's the truth that you didn't pay Gertie for sex."

Hoscomb's lips twisted. "Fine. That's why I ran from y'all. I figured you saw what I'd done and were going to arrest me for it. I might be back to my old ways, but I swear, I ain't no murderer. On the Holy Bible, I swear."

She glanced over at Brisbane, and said, "We should have Lyons check his alibi to make sure."

He nodded and dragged his hands down his face. Her sentiments exactly. For the first time that day, she let the exhaustion take over. She yawned. They were back to square one.

*

"One second!" Rylie called as she finished washing her face in the bathroom.

She rushed to the door of her motel room and found a large plastic bag filled with food, waiting for her. The delivery driver had already left.

One sniff of the food, and she realized she was actually hungry. Made sense, since she hadn't eaten all day. She glanced at the clock on the night table. It was after ten.

Slipping into her ballet flats, she went outside and knocked on the door of the room next to her. A lot of things had been niggling at her mind. She'd known she wouldn't be able to sleep. So the second she'd gotten in, she'd ordered take-out for two. Steaks. She was still feeling guilty over snapping at Michael, and so she thought a peace-offering was in order.

But there was no answer.

She knocked again, louder. Still . . . nothing.

Maybe he was asleep. It was possible that he was dead to the world, after their long day. Was he that heavy a sleeper?

She knocked again, then looked down at the food. In her mind, she conjured up a scenario—that he'd been waiting to get off so that he could meet up with that girl, Hazel Gray. They'd gotten along so well. Maybe she'd texted him, and—

*Who cares, Rylie? Really, does it matter where he is? He's not here. And that means you have to eat two steaks, yourself. Stupid.*

She trudged back to her room, swiped the key card, and went inside, feeling defeated.

The floor was gray wood laminate, the walls white, and all of the fixtures, from the beds to the chairs to the lamps were sharp angles, either rectangles or squares. It felt very cold, which was probably because of her mood.

And now, she really didn't have much of an appetite for steak.

She opened up the containers and sat in bed, picking at the French fries, watching *The Terminator* on television, and cursing herself.

She didn't just feel stupid for not telling Michael Brisbane before she ordered the feast. They hadn't made much progress in the case, and so she was antsy. It just seemed like everyone was moving forward with their lives. Everyone except her father and her.

Rylie was in a holding pattern. Her father was the same. Everything had just ended that day. And she feared things might stay that way forever, as long as her family tragedy remained unsolved.

Though she hadn't talked to her father in ages, something pulled at her. Her mother would be rolling over in her grave, right now, knowing they were estranged. It hurt to know that. Why shouldn't Rylie get in touch with him? He was the only one in the world who knew exactly what she was going through. No one, not even a sympathetic person like Michael Brisbane, could understand. Oh, he might listen to her, he might offer his sympathies, but could he ever really get it?

No.

And that made her feel even more alone than ever.

Her father, though, was there. And really just a phone call away.

Linda Hamilton was doing what she did best in that first *Terminator* movie—acting helpless and cowering behind Reese. But Rylie wasn't helpless. She took control of her destiny. She made things happen.

But what was the only thing she could think to make happen right now?

She grabbed the phone and punched in his number.

Then she sat there, staring at it, second-guessing. It was really late. Though he probably wasn't sleeping, same as her, he'd question why she called. And then they'd stumble through the conversation, with long, awkward pauses where they each ignored the elephant in the room. He wasn't the biggest talker in the world. In fact, she couldn't remember a time he'd said any more than a couple words to her.

She didn't have the energy for that.

She closed out her phone. *You're terminated.*

Then she sunk down in the bed, pulled the cover up to her chin, and made plans to hit the files again tomorrow, looking for more leads.

## CHAPTER NINETEEN

The Scarred Man pulled onto the shoulder of the interstate and let out a curse as he banged his fist against the steering wheel. Some sad country song was playing on the radio, and it only made his mood worse.

It was after one.

Late. Too late. From now until morning, the interstate was dead. If he saw twenty cars on this road between now and sun-up, it would be a lot. People just didn't travel around here during the witching hours, if they didn't have to. And young women, alone? No. That was a snowball's chance in hell.

He was too late. He'd missed his opportunity.

He lit up a cigarette and rolled down the window, letting the cold night air brace the mottled skin of his cheeks. Taking a drag, he tried to calm his shaking fingers by wrapping them around the dial and switching the radio to a more upbeat tune.

He found Billy Rae Cyrus's "Achy Breaky Heart," and kept that on, tapping his fingers on the dash. It helped, but not enough.

That was how he got, when he thought about taking his next victim. He was so excited, he could barely keep it contained. But knowing that he'd have to wait until morning made him feel like dirt. It was like a drug, and he needed his next fix.

But he still had to be smart about it. That last kill had happened too fast. He needed to stretch it out. He couldn't keep taking girl after girl, only to squander each opportunity. First of all, finding young girls who were traveling alone at night was no easy task. And secondly, the more he took, the wiser the police would get. He had to be careful, this time, which was why he hadn't wanted to wait until morning. There'd be more people out, then. More chances of getting caught.

He took a few more puffs of his cigarette, hoping that it would calm him enough so he could call it a day, go back to his house in Story Creek and then try again, tomorrow night.

No such luck. He had it in his veins. A hunger. A need. No way would he be able to wait that long.

He'd stay out here all night, if he had to. He'd take whatever risk he needed to.

Good thing the police around these parts were absolutely worthless.

But as worthless as they were, they would be on his tail, soon. He'd killed two girls in the area, so far. They were probably looking for him, now, the bumbling idiots. Thumbs up their asses, trying to figure out where he'd strike next. It'd take them a while, but they'd catch up with him. Eventually, he'd have to move on. Farther down the road. Maybe to South Dakota.

Right now, though?

Just one more. If he had one more, he'd be sated. He'd just take her tonight. Keep her until morning, until her screams died down and she had a false sense of security. Usually, that was what happened. Frantic at first, they calmed down, only to freak out once more when they realized the end was near. So if he took this girl tonight, he wouldn't kill her 'til morning. Maybe even the afternoon, if he could. Stretch it out. Maybe he could even stretch her out a few days. Kill her little by little. Make her wonder what he had up his sleeve.

*A few more minutes,* he told himself. *Just a few more minutes.*

No sooner had the thought occurred to him did he see the headlights appear in the distance, far off on the bottom of the hill. As the car drew closer, it became more and more promising. It was a little sporty car, and the color was a pale aqua.

Definitely a young woman's car.

He squinted as she passed by, trying to get a gauge on her. All he saw, in a flash, was a hand raking through long blonde hair.

She was young. And pretty. And alone.

This was it.

Flicking his cigarette out onto the dirt, he quickly threw his car into drive and took off, his heartbeat racing like the motor in his truck. As he drove, he checked himself in the mirror. *Here's your chance, you handsome devil. Don't blow it, now.*

He passed by the sign for Sheridan. Thirteen miles away. Once he reached the town, it would be too late. There was too much risk, causing an accident there. But out here, where there were no witnesses?

He pushed the gas pedal to the floor, and easily caught up with her. The Scarred Man smiled when he saw her license plate: *LV2DNCE.*

A dancer. Oh, she'd be perfect.

He licked his lips and moved forward, his headlights lining up with her back window. He moved forward until he was almost at her bumper, and saw her, peering in the rearview mirror like they always did.

This girl was a little vixen. She brake-checked him.

He slammed on his brakes. Then he laughed. "Bring it on, little girl," he said, correcting, moving back into position, right on her tail.

She brake-checked again. He could've just hit her, right then, but the name of the game was taking his time. Plus, he was having fun with this. He pounded his brake again.

She sped up a little, trying to get him off her tail, but the Scarred Man kept up with her.

This time, he swerved a little, side-to-side, toying with her.

She powered down her window and stuck a thin arm out, with long graceful fingers. At first, he thought she was motioning him to go around. But then he realized she was giving him the finger.

His permanent smile widened. He was absolutely going to love this.

After a little bit of cat and mouse, they sailed past a sign that said, *SHERIDAN- 5 Miles.*

It was time to strike.

He was ready. Gripping his steering wheel, he made like he was going to pass her on the left. As he did, he got a better look at her face in the driver's-side mirror. A waterfall of platinum blonde hair, pink glossy lips, and dangling gold earrings.

The Scarred Man flashed back to that night. His father's wild eyes. The indifferent look of the woman in the sportscar, who'd given him the finger and pushed, pushed, pushed all the wrong buttons until his dad had no choice but to break. After that, the screaming in the cab. The screeching of tires. Bracing himself for whatever came next.

This woman? She was perfect. He had to get her.

He had to be careful—her car was a tiny thing, and he didn't want to cause any major damage. What if the accident killed her? No, he had to orchestrate this perfectly, so she wasn't hurt, just a little dazed.

He moved a closer, a little closer, and then . . . impact.

By now, he was used to exactly what would happen next. He held tightly—but not too tightly—to the steering wheel, allowing his truck to ricochet from the hit, then taking his foot off the gas and steering into the pressure that seemed to want to make him veer wildly off the road. Easy peasy. No problem at all.

However, the same could not be said for the girl. In the next second after the collision, he gained control of his car and continued a straight path in the fast lane. As he did, he looked through his passenger-side window to see her swerving off toward the shoulder, her eyes wide and frightened, her hands, with their long, dangerous claw-like fingernails, scrabbling frantically to maintain control of the wheel.

But she couldn't. In the next second, her car crashed through the guardrail and plummeted down the embankment, bounding over the rough terrain, kicking up a cloud of dust as it dug itself into the long grass there. The sound was thunderous—almost as loud as his own heartbeat. It steered to the right and came to a juddering halt.

He quickly slammed on his brakes and pulled over to the side of the highway. Before the truck had come to a full stop, he threw it into park and pushed open the door. He looked up and down the interstate. No headlights to be seen. Luck was on his side.

He jogged down the embankment to the wreck, humming to himself. The front of the sportscar had gotten crushed from its impact with the guardrail, so only one headlight was working, its glow and the moonlight illuminating the inflated airbag through the windshield. There was a thin plume of smoke rising into the night air from under the hood, but other than that, everything was completely silent. He went around to the driver's side door and peered into the window. The woman was slumped toward the door, her hair falling in her face.

He pulled open the door. "Hello," he said pleasantly.

Her head lolled toward him, and when her eyes opened, they were bleary, unfocused. "Where—what happened?"

Good. She wasn't going to scream. She'd be easy. He loved it when they had temporary amnesia. It allowed him to toy with them even more.

"You've been in an accident," he said, reaching in. When he leaned in, he smelled male cologne. She was probably coming home from a boyfriend's place. He removed her seatbelt. "Let's get you out of here and take you somewhere so you can get checked out, okay?"

She nodded, dazed, and pulled her body out from under the steering wheel. She was a tiny thing, probably less than five feet tall, wearing tight jeans and a tank-top. He lifted her up into his arms, and carried her easily up the embankment toward his truck.

It was only when he paused at the back of his truck to lower the tailgate that she roused, lifting her head off his shoulder and looking around. Still groggy, she blinked hard a few times, and looked up at him.

That was when she started to scream.

“There, there,” he said in a soothing voice, finally succeeding in undoing the clasp on the tailgate and lowering it. She looked down, frantic, as he set her down and tried to slide her in.

“What are you . . .? No!” She began to kick. Her hair tangled in his fingers. Her high heel dug into his hip.

She flailed, her face contorting into an ugly visage, her eyes wide with fear, despite his assurances. He grabbed her wrists tight and shoved her back, then pulled up the tailgate and locked the tonneau cover, effectively sealing her inside.

Her muffled screams rose up, anyway.

He’d take her to his house, now, where no one could hear her. He’d make himself breakfast—scrambled eggs and toast—and let her scream and scream until she was tired out. And this time, he would make some lovely plans to enjoy her. To take it slow.

Yes. He couldn’t wait.

# CHAPTER TWENTY

The following morning, still half-asleep, Rylie finished getting ready for the day and looked at herself in the mirror.

She looked terrible. The bags under her eyes were big enough for a trip to Japan. There were wrinkles around her mouth, too. Laugh lines, ironic, considering she didn't do very much of that anymore. She rubbed at them, wondering when she started looking so *old.* Were the best years of her life really behind her?

*If so, I can't wait to see what the worst years have in store for me.*

It was only six-thirty in the morning, but that didn't matter. She hardly slept at all. Too much on her mind. Now, she wanted to get moving.

The hotel room still smelled like last night's steak dinner, most of which had gone in the trash. The smell was suffocating, making her stomach roil. She grabbed her things, took one last look around the hotel room to make sure she hadn't forgotten anything, and stepped out.

Then she knocked on the neighboring door.

This time, she got an answer. "One sec," a groggy voice said from inside. A moment later, the door opened, and she found a sleepy-looking Michael Brisbane, wearing nothing but boxers and a t-shirt, staring back at her, scratching his stubbled chin. Quickly, she averted her eyes, feeling awkward.

"Well, don't you look like crap," he said.

She snorted and smoothed her hair. "Thanks for noticing. I didn't sleep last night. And you think you look any better?"

"Well . . . I did sleep. I *was* sleeping, until you . . ." He rubbed his eyes and looked back in his room. "Oh, shit. Did I oversleep?"

He left the door open and went back inside. She hovered in the doorway as he went to his night table and picked up his phone. She explained, "Well, I'd like to get on the road, because I've had a couple ideas and think we should—"

"It's six-thirty," he mumbled, falling back into bed. "Too early."

She'd expected him to say that. "That's fine. If you don't want to come with me, I'll just go out on my own and—"

He rolled onto his side and propped himself up on his elbow. "Where do you think you'll go? Everything's closed right now. It's dead."

"The station's open. I'll go there and review the files."

He let out a groan and said, "We've been through those files, again and again. What new information are you expecting to uncover at six-thirty in the morning?"

She shrugged. "Well, you might be a little more awake if you hadn't gone out last night," she suggested nonchalantly. "Where did you go?"

He sat up. "Go? Nowhere. I got into the hotel, took a shower, and then crashed."

She stood there, feeling silly about that earlier thought that he was traipsing around Wyoming with Hazel Gray. Of course, it made total sense that he'd take a shower to wash the nasty business of the day off of him. She'd thought about doing it, too.

"Oh," she said with a shrug. "I stopped by with steak for you last night, but you didn't answer."

"You did?" His eyes widened. "Sorry. I didn't hear you knock."

"It's okay. I thought you might've gone out."

He laughed. "Where? Not like there's much night-life happening around here after midnight. Unless I wanted to go back to Willy's. Which . . . no thanks. I don't think they liked us much, there."

She wandered in and sat on one of the square chairs. "Yeah. I don't know. I thought maybe you went for a walk because you couldn't sleep."

He shook his head. "Damn. I can't believe I missed it. Probably the only time I'd be anti-steak would be when I'm asleep." He patted his stomach. "You just reminded me how starving I am."

She smiled. "Well . . . if you get dressed, we can go down the street for breakfast? I saw an IHOP at the exit."

"That's a plan," he said, standing, grabbing his duffle bag, and stumbling off toward the bathroom.

She pointed to the door. "I can wait out—"

"No. Stay there. I'll just be a minute."

He closed the door and she scrolled through her phone, thinking. Brisbane was probably right. They'd been through those files numerous times. And the more they dug, the more questions they had. It was probably their best bet to look into the murder of Erin Littlefeather, since it had just happened recently and they had a body.

She opened up her phone and looked up Erin Littlefeather online, trying to see if she was active on social media. She did have an Instagram account, but it was marked as private. If need be, they could open it up and research who her friends were, to see if they could make a connection that way.

But that didn't seem right. There was absolutely nothing to connect Lila Garrity, a young married woman from Sheridan, and Erin Littlefeather, a high school girl from Banner, except their method of death. They'd both been driving, alone, at night, on that dreaded highway, and had been forced off the road by a vehicle with black paint.

So that meant the killer was likely choosing these victims at random, and that both women were just in the wrong place at the wrong time.

And that meant looking into the women's backgrounds wouldn't really do any good. What they needed to do, instead, was get out there. Get as many eyes on the road as possible. Something that wasn't really easy to do, considering how few police they had, to cover such a large stretch of road.

Just as her legs itched with the need to move, to get out there, the door opened and Michael appeared, freshly showered and shaved and ready to go. "Let's get out of here," he said, slipping into his shoulder holster and grabbing his jacket and phone.

As they drove over to the IHOP, she told him of her plan. "I think we need to see if we can enlist other police stations to keep an eye on the road, as much as possible. If he's taken these two girls within twenty-four hours, it won't be long until he tries it again, probably on the same road."

Brisbane snorted. "That's a tall order. Most of these police departments are one-or-two member outfits."

"I know, I know. But we have to keep eyes on the road somehow."

"That's a lot of road to be eyeing."

She sighed as they pulled into the parking lot. "I guess it's probably wishful thinking. But I think that's why I didn't sleep last night. I keep thinking like there's something more we should be doing. And I'm not doing it, holed up in a hotel."

"What'd you want to do? Camp out along the side of the road? You think you'll be more useful that way?"

"Maybe . . ." She was only half-joking.

He stared at the dashboard and nodded. "Look. I get it. I didn't sleep all that well last night, either, turning over the facts of the case. But I remind myself that I'm no good as the walking dead, and I need that shut-eye in order to perform well at my job. That's just what you need to do. You're no good to anyone, falling asleep on the beat."

"I guess," she said. "I haven't slept well in ages."

"It's easy to take these cases personally. You hear of a victim that reminds you of your best girlfriend from college or an old boyfriend, and you start to feel overly invested. You have to step back. Getting too close to a case is a good way to cloud your judgement."

*Too close.* She ran those words over in her head. Yes, she was, automatically, with every kidnapping and murder case she came across. She couldn't help it. Every one of them made her think of her own tragedy. She couldn't not be invested. And so maybe her judgement was a little clouded. Maybe it was good to have Michael there, to tell her when she was losing her grip.

They went inside the IHOP, which was busy, considering they hadn't seen another soul since leaving the empty motel.

"I haven't been in one of these places in ages. I'm getting a Rooty Tooty," he said as the waitress led them to a corner booth.

"Well, it's your treat, since I bought dinner last night."

They slid into the booth at opposite ends. "Hey. I didn't even get a bite of that great dinner of yours."

"It was great. Really good," she said, rubbing it in.

"You had both?"

"I did," she lied, patting her stomach, unable to resist teasing him. "I'm really not even all that hungry."

"Now you're making me feel bad. So you starved me all day yesterday and went back to your room and ate two meals. Is that it?"

She shrugged. "I tried to share."

He grabbed his heart. "You're killing me. Right here."

"Yeah, well, the amount of cholesterol in those steaks is probably killing *me* right there, too."

"Wow. I didn't know you had a sense of humor," he said, mock-surprised.

She smiled. She had to admit that most of the time, she never really felt in a joking mood. Not just around him, but around everyone. But it felt good to be able to use that muscle, like normal people.

"Now tell me. How hard did you really knock? You probably wanted both steaks to yourself. Just to torture me. Admit it."

She almost laughed. But then his phone started to ring, and he picked it up.

"Brisbane, here." He glanced at her and tensed, and she remembered just why they were here. It was probably Lyons, calling, since Officer Lyons and Brisbane had become close friends. "Yeah. What happened?"

She leaned forward, trying to hear, but the most she could make out on the other end were a few random broken syllables. "What is it?"

He held up a finger to her and spoke into the receiver. "Okay, yeah. Where?"

She tapped the table nervously as the waitress came by to fill their coffee mugs. She hadn't even cracked her menu. She put up her hand. "Give us a moment, please. We might have had a change of plans."

The waitress nodded. "Sure thing."

"We'll be right there," Brisbane said, ending the call.

"What is it?" she asked, even before he'd pressed the button.

He shuffled his backside to the end of the bench seat, and she followed suit. "That was Lyons. They found another crashed car. This one happened last night. Not too far from where we were last night, at Willy's."

Rylie stiffened. So she'd been right. Had she been out there, on the road, she might've seen something. No wonder she couldn't sleep. Another young girl was probably going through hell right now, and she'd been sleeping in a comfy bed. It didn't seem right. "Was it a girl?"

He nodded as they headed out the door. "They already ran the plates, and it appears the driver of the car is another young female."

"Oh, no," she murmured, climbing into the cab of her truck. "Tell me where to go."

"Get on the interstate going south, and I'll tell you from there."

She surged out of the parking space, nearly colliding with another car, coming into the lot. The driver laid on the horn and gave her the finger. Ignoring it, she punched the gas, speeding onto the road in the direction of route 86.

"Whoa," he said. "Let's be careful. They just found it. It'll still be there when we get there."

She shook her head. "Don't you get it? This is our fault. We always need to be on the job. When we take our eyes off the road, stuff like this happens."

*

Michael Brisbane held on for dear life as Rylie careened onto the interstate, her speed quickly reaching over 100 miles per hour. He dug his fingers into the armrest and tried to remain calm, but he had to admit, she was scaring him.

For a second, back there, he'd thought she was loosening up. She'd been in almost a lighthearted mood, smiling and joking with him. He thought that over a couple of coffees and Rooty Tooty Fresh and Fruity breakfasts, they might bond over their pasts. Build trust. Become friends.

But then he'd gotten the call.

He knew why Lyons called him, instead of her. She was intense. Like now. She had only one mode—and that was hyper-speed.

"Hey," he said, as gently as he could. "You can't seriously think that us not being on the road to catch this guy last night is our fault?"

"It is," she insisted. "Definitely. We were so close. We should've . . . I don't know . . ."

"That's the thing about this job. We don't know. We can only act on the evidence we have. And we didn't have any evidence to find this creep. But we'll get it. And then—"

"Tell that to the girl whose car was hit last night," she snapped, swerving into the fast lane and passing another car like it was standing still.

He gripped the armrest. "Listen to me. If you keep thinking all this shit is your fault, you're going to burn out. Crack. Go crazy before you hit retirement age. No FBI agent could handle that. You know that, right?"

She didn't answer. She stared straight ahead.

Maybe she didn't know it. But it was too late. Before he could say any more, she pulled up to the side of the road, where the police cars had gathered.

They saw the aqua-colored sportscar from the road, stranded in the middle of a level field of yellow grass. By the time Michael removed his seatbelt, Rylie was out the door and already halfway down the embankment.

When he got to the crime scene, she was already talking to Lyons.

"The driver is registered to one Ivy Benson, twenty-one, who lives north of Sheridan. We're trying to get in touch with family and friends to see if anyone spoke to her or knows where she was coming from.

Maybe she'd been partying it up at a local bar and drank a little too much, but I think—"

"That would be a pretty big coincidence."

"Yeah. It's too similar to those two other cases—pretty young girl, crashed her car, and now she's nowhere to be found."

Brisbane pulled out his pad and pen and wrote down the girl's name. "Any other evidence left behind?"

He motioned up toward the road. "There were some tire marks in the dirt on the side of the road. Looked like they belonged to a big pickup truck, not that it helps narrow things down much, around here. Also a couple of footprints. Big, cowboy boots. Male. That doesn't help narrow things down much, either, I'm afraid."

Rylie nodded and marched over to the crashed vehicle. She peered inside the driver's side door for a moment, but then went back to the rear bumper.

"Bris!" she shouted, stooping in front of the tail-light. "Here it is again. Black paint."

Michael Brisbane jogged over to meet her, noting the fuzzy dice hanging from the rearview mirror, the stuffed animals in the back window of the car, and the LUV2DNCE license plate. The car screamed YOUNG NAÏVE FEMALE from miles away.

But sure enough, a substantial dent was there above the broken tail-light, just as obvious as day.

"We should definitely be having Beeker get us a list of black pick-ups registered in the area."

Rylie nodded. "Might be a lot, though. " Rylie went to the front of the car and looked in. "No sign of blood or struggle. No footprints down here?" she asked Lyons.

Lyons said, "The grass was pretty thick. No footprints. No evidence at all."

Rylie turned away and walked off, on her own, toward the woods. She looked pissed. Probably taking this all way too hard. No wonder she'd left Seattle. If she kept going like this, taking everything this hard, she probably wouldn't make it another year in the force.

"Hey," he said, jogging after her. She'd stopped now, and was facing a line of ponderosa pines bordering a rusted old post-and-wire fence. "So here's what I think. I think this is good. Now it tells us for sure that this dude is targeting young women, traveling solo. So I think if we go back to the office, we can separate out all the files of young women from the area. That'll narrow things down. And then—"

"And then what?" she said, shaking her head. "You're right. We've gone through those files over and over and found nothing. Even if we did find other murders, those women are gone. It won't bring them back. Maybe we have to stop looking at what happened in the past and focus on what we can do in the present. But I don't know what that is."

He had to admit, the idea of going through those files again, after everything, felt like an exercise in futility. He'd gone through them so many times, he had parts of them memorized. "Well . . . you know what they say . . . the past is prologue. And what other choice do we have?"

She glanced at him. "That's very Shakespearean of you. Fine. I guess if that's our only option, we'll go through once more, pull out all the women under the age of twenty-five and give them another look. See where that gets us."

He gave her the double thumbs up. "Let's do this."

## CHAPTER TWENTY ONE

An hour later, Rylie sat in the cramped break room at the police station, with a slightly smaller pile of files in front of her than before. These were the files of incidents that had happened to young women while driving alone. She pored over them, trying to find any connection to the recent cases. Brisbane also had a stack, and was carefully paging through files while polishing off his Hardee's pancake breakfast.

Beeker had arrived, too, and was now sitting on the floor for lack of table space, back against a trash can, crisscross-applesauce, checking the files on his trusty computer.

The tiny room was so full, the stench of old coffee and maple syrup so powerful, Rylie swallowed the nausea in the back of her throat for the third time that hour and tried to concentrate.

No . . . she felt it. It was coming up.

She pushed the folder aside, climbed over Beeker's legs, and rushed to the sink, where she stood, sure she'd begin dry heaving, much to her embarrassment. The last thing she needed was her associates thinking she might be pregnant. As if that was even possible.

But the feeling passed.

She found a paper cup and filled it with water from the faucet, then sucked it down. When she turned around, Michael was studying her curiously.

"You should've had some breakfast," he said to her, offering a grease-stained bag. "Want a hash brown?"

She shook her head. "It's the smell of all that grease that has me feeling sick to begin with."

"Yeah, but it can't feel good, on an empty stomach, to—"

"Trust me. I ate two steaks last night, remember? My stomach is *far* from empty." It wasn't true; she'd thrown most of it away, but the last thing she wanted to do now was eat. There was too much work to do.

He leaned back, lifted a shade, and cracked a window. Immediately, cool air filtered in. "Better?"

It was. She nodded and sat back down, just as Officer Lyons came in. "I have news, agents. About the kidnapping victim, Ivy Benson."

"Lay it on us," Brisbane said, not looking up.

"So she was heading home from her boyfriend's place. He's in a dorm at Casper College, and he said good night to her and walked her to her car at around midnight. She goes to Sheridan College on a dance scholarship. Her roommate called the campus police when she didn't show up and missed her morning dance practice. She said she spoke to her on the phone while she was en route and she mentioned something about a creepy guy in a truck, on her ass. Following her."

Rylie exchanged a look with her partner. "That's our guy," she said. "I knew it . . ."

Brisbane nodded. "Yeah . . . but let's not get carried away. Lila's still out there, and now Ivy . . . he's being brazen, and that means he's going to get sloppy. He's going to trip up and someone will have seen something."

"Lyons, change that APB we put out yesterday to include any black pick-up trucks driven by a male on Interstate 86," Rylie said. "Especially trucks with front-end damage, no matter how slight."

"Okay," he said doubtfully, "But that's gonna keep us real busy."

"I know. But I don't care if we get a thousand tips. It's better right now that we play it safe and talk to as many people as we can. I want the police to stay alert to this threat."

"Got it," he said, spinning and heading out to follow her orders.

Beeker tapped away on the computer and said, "I can bring up a list of any black pick-ups serviced at local shops for front-end damage, if you want?"

She shook her head. "It hasn't been long enough between incidents. I don't think he'd have time to have his truck serviced in between. Can you instead just get me a list of black pick-ups registered in this area?"

He whistled. "Sure can, but dude . . . that's going to be a mighty big list."

"Yes, I know, but I'd rather—"

"Wait," Michael said. "Can you cross reference the data in the FBI cold case files with the list of black pick-ups?"

Beeker held up a finger. "That, I can do. One second."

"The cold case files that include any young female, aged eighteen to twenty-five, in either Sheridan or Johnson county, Wyoming, for the past. . . five years?" he continued, looking at her for confirmation.

She nodded. "Any violent crime committed by a male."

"Yeah. Five years. Violent crime. Male perpetrator," he added.

Rylie sat back in her seat. That was a good idea. She wished she'd thought of it. But right now, she was seeing double from looking at the files, not to mention that her stomach was queasy, and it wasn't even ten in the morning. Anything to make the job easier, she was all for.

Beeker tapped away at his keyboard, his fingers moving over the keys like lightning as they both watched and waited, the folders in front of them forgotten.

"Aha," he said, jumping to his feet and setting his laptop on the table between them. "Now we are cooking with gas, guys. I think this list ought to narrow things down considerably. These names here are of anyone who has registered a black pick-up in the county, and whose name matches someone who committed a violent crime in the area in the past five years."

Rylie looked at the first one. "Mark J. Smith from Arvada."

Beeker tapped the touchpad and clicked on the name. "Says here he was arrested for domestic abuse. Kidnapping." He scrolled. "Jeez. Guy has a long rap sheet."

That sounded promising. "Okay, we should look into h—"

"Whoops. Wait. Forget it. He's deceased. Died last year. He was eighty-four."

Brisbane frowned. "Can we narrow down the list to *living* people, Beek?"

"Calm down, Bris, I'm on it," he said, doing a little magic with his fingers. The next time they looked, the list was even shorter. There were only eight names.

She pointed at the first name. "Reginald Bukowski. What about him?"

He clicked on the name. "This guy's got a pretty long rap sheet, too." He scrolled down. "But . . . looks like he moved to Arizona a year ago. He was arrested there, too, for kidnapping."

"Next," Brisbane said, dragging his hands down his face.

"Bennett Hoscomb?"

"Already checked," Rylie said quickly. "Move on. Next?"

One by one, they went through the list, eliminating suspects for whatever reason. They were already incarcerated, or out of town, or incapacitated in some other way. After the next few names, Rylie tilted her head back and stared at the ceiling. "Maybe this is a waste of time. Our guy might not have even been previously charged with any crimes. He might be new to this area."

Brisbane shook his head. "No. I think we're getting closer. Keep going."

Beeker squinted at the screen. "Okay . . . Buck Finch?"

"Buck . . . Finch?" Brisbane said, leaning forward. "Why does that name sound familiar?"

Beeker clicked on the man's name. It brought up a young guy in his mid-thirties who looked like he was being photographed for his budding modeling career, instead of a mugshot. Even in the harsh, unforgiving light of the police camera, he was undeniably handsome, with tattoos up his neck, and a piercing, blue-eyed gaze.

"Oh . . .," Rylie said, unable to tear her eyes from the photo.

"I know that guy . . .," Brisbane said, slapping his knee. "He's a pro race car driver. Or at least, he was number one with a bullet to go pro. That was years ago. Whatever happened to him?"

"Apparently nothing good, if he's on this list." Rylie raised an eyebrow. "You a NASCAR fan?"

"Rally racing," he corrected, giving her a disgusted look. "It's a superior sport."

"Okay. No clue what that is," she said with a shrug, leaning in to read more about the potential suspect. "Scroll down."

Beeker obliged as Brisbane went on. "Most people are all rah-rah about NASCAR, but the thing is, rally racing is far more challenging and exciting. It's on a public road, usually dirt, and the drivers don't usually know the course before starting the race, instead of going around and around in a loop five-hundred times."

She waved him off. "Interesting," she mumbled, pointing at the screen. "Says here he lives in Sheridan. Has a lot of drunk and disorderlies on his rap sheet. That probably has something to do with his meteoric fall from the racing circuit. From the looks of things, he's a raging alcoholic."

Beeker scrolled down more. "Get this. He killed his wife."

"What?" Rylie leaned forward. This was looking better and better. "He did only a year of prison and got time off for good behavior? I think we might need to pay this guy a visit."

"No, wait. Now I know what I remember Buck from. He killed his wife, but . . .," He grabbed his phone and typed something in. "Here. Look."

He thrust his phone in front of Rylie. She read:

*SHERIDAN RALLY CAR DRIVER PLEADS GUILTY IN WIFE'S DEATH*

*Sheridan—William "Buck" Finch, long celebrated as the area's most promising rally car driver, has pleaded guilty to manslaughter in the death of his wife of nine years, Barbara Finch. The judge has sentenced him to a prison term of five years.*

*According to police, shortly after one AM on the evening of September 30th, Finch pulled out of his driveway on Horned Butte Road, and struck Barbara Finch, who was standing behind the vehicle. Finch then drove away. A neighbor found the victim in the early morning hours and called an ambulance. Finch was pronounced dead at the scene.*

*At sentencing, Finch spoke and expressed remorse. "I loved my wife and these have been some of the darkest days of my life. I miss her, every day. I don't remember it. I was drunk. I wish I could take that day back, but I can't. I know that this is all the fault of my drinking, and that I have a problem. I resolve to get help."*

Rylie shook her head. "Oh, God, he just ran over his wife in the driveway of his house and left her there. What a great man. Sure, he loves her."

Beeker laughed bitterly. "And so much for resolving to get help. Most of these drunk and disorderlies are from *after* he got out of prison."

Rylie leaned over and made a mental note of Buck Finch's address. It was a promising lead, and they needed to jump on it, as fast as they could.

# CHAPTER TWENTY TWO

From his seated place at the breakroom table, Michael watched as Rylie filled up a commuter cup of coffee. He noticed that as she did, her fingers shook. It might have been because she'd had nothing to eat, but Michael had a feeling it was something more than that.

Something was niggling at him, but it only solidified as he watched his partner, gathering her things so that they could interrogate Buck Finch. She was acting rashly. Not thinking things through. Shooting first, asking questions later. That could be dangerous.

And why? Well, she wouldn't say why. She was a closed book. He couldn't see what made her tick, because she wouldn't let him, but Michael had the feeling there was something there. And he needed to put the reins on it.

As she fixed the lid on the cup, she glanced at him. "Are you coming, or not?"

"Whoa . . .," he said shaking his head. "I think we need to step back. I don't think we should go yet. There are still a few more names on the list, and—"

"And there are two kidnapped girls, out there. We don't have a minute to waste."

"But with Buck Finch? You really think he's our guy?"

She nodded. "Obviously. It makes perfect sense. He killed his wife. He loved her, didn't mean to do it. Maybe he had a mental break, and now he's going after women who are her age, in order to compensate."

Michael stared at her, trying to get that theory to fit in his mind. "You think that makes sense?"

"You have any better ideas?"

He didn't. Still, there were holes in her theory, too big to ignore. "Listen, Wolf. Okay, yeah, he's a drunk. And he made mistakes he probably can't forgive himself for. But look at his rap sheet. He's still an alcoholic. *That's* his way of coping with his guilt. You really think a raging alcoholic would be able to perpetrate those crimes, kidnap those girls without leaving any evidence behind?"

She hitched both shoulders. “I don’t know. But that’s why we’re going to talk to him. To find out.”

“On what basis?”

“Do I need to spell it out for you?” She held up fingers, one by one. “One, he lives nearby. Two, he drives a black pick-up. Three, he has a rap sheet. And four, he had a known history of past crimes involving women. Isn’t that enough for you?”

He shook his head. “I don’t think so.”

“Okay, then what about this? I have a hunch, and my hunches are usually right.”

He kept shaking his head. “Sorry. I get hunches, too, and with this guy? My hunch is that he has nothing to do with this crime.”

“We should still check him out.”

“Later. After we’ve exhausted all our other options.” He pointed at the computer.

She just stared at him, disappointment in her face. “Wait. So what are you saying? You don’t want to go?”

“No. I don’t think we should. Not yet. I think we should look through the other options, one by one, and make a decision then.”

“And I think,” she said, putting a hand on her hip, “that if we do that, we’re just wasting time when we could be apprehending the guy and saving those girls.”

“If he’s not our guy, and frankly, I don’t see any reason to think he is, then that would be wasting time,” he said, trying to be as gentle as possible.

It didn’t work. Her mouth fell into a straight line. She stuck out her chin and shrugged. “Fine. You can pussy-foot around all you want, waiting to be sure before you pounce. But I don’t work that way. I take risks, and they pay off.”

*Pussy foot around?* Really? Is that what she thought about him? That he played it too safe? To hell with that. He was a good agent. And her implying otherwise?

She’d just stepped over the line.

Michael had almost forgotten Beeker was there until he suddenly spoke up. “Uh, guys. You know, I can go through these last few possible suspects, if you want to—”

“No.” His gaze was fastened on Rylie’s. “I’m staying here, and I’ll go over the remaining suspects.”

She scowled at him. "So I guess I'm going to go interview our suspect alone," she said, flipping her hair as she turned and stalked out of the room.

He watched the door, long after she'd disappeared. He didn't know why. She was too obstinate. She'd made her decision. She wouldn't be coming back. And she sure as hell wouldn't admit he was right.

She was infuriating.

But he sure as hell hoped she knew what she was doing. If, on the off-chance he really was the killer, and something happened to her, he'd never forgive himself.

He couldn't think about that now. He settled back into his chair and looked at Beeker's computer. "What's the next one?"

*

Rylie drove to the address that she'd scribbled hastily on a piece of paper, muttering curses to herself the whole time. How dare her partner question her logic?

After all, she hadn't just pulled the name out of a hat. There was good reason to suspect Buck Finch of this crime, and that meant acting on the information as soon as they got it. Not playing around. So what was his problem? Why did he always have to be so damned careful? If she'd acted that way in Seattle, she wouldn't have caught half as many perpetrators as she had.

She tried not to think of the way he'd looked at her, before she left. For the first time, Michael Brisbane wasn't that happy-go-lucky, everything's-fine kind of guy. He'd looked almost *angry*.

Then she cursed herself for caring what he thought. It didn't matter one lick to her if Michael Brisbane was angry with her. She was used to pissing off people. And it didn't matter if he wasn't here. She'd never wanted a partner to begin with. She preferred being alone. As far as she was concerned, this was perfect. She could make much more headway without him.

So then why was she so upset about the whole situation? She should've been happy. This was what she wanted.

She shook her head. *Forget it, Rylie. It doesn't matter. Just move on.*

Main Street in downtown Sheridan was a cute little walk back in time, with charming storefronts, an old movie house, five and dimes, little restaurants and cafés, all set against a backdrop of the snow-covered Bighorn Mountains.

She'd been here, once, long ago, during that RV trip she'd rather have forgotten. She remembered walking up the street with her sister and Kiki, stopping to get ice cream at a place with a big cartoon buffalo on the front. As she drove, she looked around for it, but couldn't see it anywhere.

Buck Finch's place was over a corner coffee shop called Lulu's Bakery and Beanery. She pulled into one of the spots at the storefront, just as a couple of college-aged students in skull-caps with backpacks slung over their shoulders came walking out, nursing their caffeinated drinks. The smell of coffee and sugary treats made her mouth water, but she didn't want to waste the time going in.

Unlike Michael Brisbane, she understood when time was of the essence. She needed to talk to Buck Finch as soon as possible.

The entrance to the apartments was through a separate doorway, behind the café. There was a sign—*SHERIDAN EFFICIENCY APARTMENTS—1 and 2 BR.* She followed an arrow on the sign down a narrow alley, and climbed the steps up to a long hallway, with four apartments, knocking on the door to number 4.

The was no answer.

She knocked again, harder, and that was when the door gave way slightly, pushing open an inch. "Hello?" she called out. "Buck Finch?"

Again, there was no answer. But the door was open, inviting a look inside. She saw cluttered bookcase, filled with trophies, likely racing trophies. There was a photograph of a man in a racing helmet, standing next to his rally car. At least she knew she had the right place, but where was Finch? The apartment was dark, but she could hear voices and smell the scent of stale cigarettes and old garbage. Lights danced in the darkness, pale blue.

Someone was in there.

She pushed the door open just a bit more, so she could stick her head through. "Hello?"

Rylie had expected a bit of a bachelor pad—unkempt and without a woman's touch. But this was beyond that. There was trash on every inch of the floor—mostly beer cans and liquor bottles, but also fast-food napkins and boxes, piles of laundry, broken glass, smashed furniture. It was like a riot for the eyes—everywhere she looked, she found something more horrifying. The place looked like it had been ransacked, and the stench was overpowering, making her eyes water and her stomach roil even more.

Craning her neck to look around the cramped, dirty apartment, she noticed the old box television, among the debris. It was on, set to some old television sit-com with a canned laugh-track. She scanned to the shapeless, overstuffed sofa with the tears in the cushion and noticed a lumpy form, laid out on it.

Was that a person?

Yes, as she squinted in the darkness, she could make out the individual features. The jeans, the curve of the back, long, unkempt hair. It was a man, lying on his stomach—his one exposed cheek was covered in thick stubble. His arm hung down from the sofa, fingers scraping the ground. For a moment, she thought he might be dead.

Then he let out one long, obnoxious snore.

She took a step in, wondering if he'd wake, and kept walking closer, pushing aside debris with her feet. At one point, something caught her eye, scurrying near her shoe. She looked down and winced at a cockroach, the size of her big toe.

"Ugh," she said aloud, Brisbane's words coming to her. *You really think a raging alcoholic would be able to perpetrate those crimes, kidnap those girls without leaving any evidence behind?*

Those words hit her hard, pulling at her. This guy couldn't even find a trash can. How could he murder those girls?

Still, she kept moving closer. Even if she was wrong, she could still do something right and eliminate him as a suspect. Even if he wasn't the killer, she could still move the case forward, which was more than Brisbane was doing now.

She shoved aside some more trash and finally reached the couch. There was a half-empty bottle of Budweiser near his hand, and when she leaned over him, the smell of booze and body odor was stronger than ever.

"Mr. Finch?" she asked.

Nothing. He didn't even move.

She reached over and nudged him, touching his sweat-stained undershirt at the shoulder. "Hello?"

She nudged harder.

"Mr. Finch?" Now, she was shouting.

Without warning, he sprang up and advanced on her, gripping the beer bottle in his hand. She stumbled back, falling to her backside, her elbows cushioned by the trash.

"Who the hell are you?" he snarled, his eyes on fire. Holding the amber bottle by its neck, he slammed it up against the side of the television, breaking it into a lethal weapon as he stalked toward her.

He reached her and stooped over her, grabbing her by the shoulder and holding the sharp point of his new weapon up to her throat. It pressed into her skin, threatening to tear open a life-ending wound.

"I told you already! I don't got anymore. The well is dry. You get it?"

She met his eyes with defiance, holding her body stiff so the sharp instrument wouldn't puncture her skin. "I don't know what you're talking about. I'm Rylie Wolf from the FBI."

He stared at her for a moment before scoffing. "The hell you are. They don't hire *girls*."

She carefully pushed aside her jacket to reveal the credentials at her belt. "I assure you, they do."

His eyes drifted down to the badge, and seemed to widen slightly. He fumbled for a second, faltering, and it was in that second that Rylie knew she had to act. She swiped his arm away, then shoved him in the chest with all of her might, causing him to lose his grip on the bottle. It skittered to the floor as he fell backwards, dazed. His hair fell in his face, and he let out a moan of pain as he stumbled to try to retrieve it.

"What the . . ."

In that instant, she pulled out her gun and leveled it at him. "Stop right there, Buck Finch. Don't move."

He turned to stare down the barrel of her gun, and slowly raised his hands. "What the hell do you want from me?"

"Right now, I just want to talk to you," she said. "So sit down and don't try anything stupid. You understand?"

# CHAPTER TWENTY THREE

Rylie cleared a space off at the kitchenette in the middle of the studio apartment, and sat down. As she did, her phone began to ring with a call from Brisbane.

She didn't have time for that bull. He was probably calling to see if she'd made any headway in the case, and if not, rub her face in it. She let it go right to voicemail.

"Like I said," Buck Finch said, leaning against the sink full of dirty dishes and raking his hands through his greasy hair. "I'm sorry, Agent. Can I get you something? Some . . ."

He opened the fridge, which was empty except for a few condiments and terrible, moldy smell that somehow outdid the other smells in the apartment. He closed the door quickly and looked around.

"Water? I can get you water. I'd offer tea, but . . ." He laughed mournfully. "I'm sorry, I've been a little busy and haven't cleaned the place this week."

*This week? It looks like it's never been cleaned.*

"No, it's fine," she said, moving some old Chinese food containers away from her, a bit worried they might avalanche back on top of her. "I don't need anything. I just wanted to ask you a few questions."

"All right." He sat down across from her, looked in a greasy bag and grimaced, then wiped his hands on his ratty undershirt and sniffled. "I'll try. I'm feeling a little under the weather. Think I'm just getting over a cold. Sorry."

The drinking until he lost consciousness probably wasn't helping, but she had more important things to deal with. "It's all right. How long have you been living here?"

He looked around. "A year, maybe? Shithole, isn't it?" He shrugged. "But the rent's okay. I'm between jobs right now, so money's a little tight."

"You haven't been working?"

"No. Not since . . .." He gnawed on his lip. "You probably already know. I got out of prison a year ago."

She nodded.

"I used to live in a nice place. Out in the country. Nice development. Had acreage. But then . . ."

She nodded. "I understand. Your wife died."

He hung his head. "Yeah. She did. She was pregnant, too, with my son. Did you know that?"

Rylie shook her head. "No. I didn't."

"I don't know if it was a boy. I hoped it was. She was only six weeks along. My lawyers told me I was lucky I wasn't charged with double homicide. But I don't feel lucky at all." He stared at the table in front of him and drummed his fingers on its surface. "Not at all."

She couldn't help but feel a little bad for him. "I'm very sorry."

He looked up at her. "I'm sure you already know what happened. I wish I could say the same but I'd been drinking for a long time. When I got into rallying, it was like that. You drive hard, then you drink hard. That's all we ever did. Ever since I was fifteen. It's just like I told the police, the day after. I honestly can't remember a damn thing about that night."

"You don't remember *anything*?"

"No. I wish I did. I thought I passed out and went to bed, and the next thing I know, I was lying on my front lawn, covered in my own puke, and my neighbors were standing over me, telling me I'd hit her with my car. By the time I came to and dragged my ass to the hospital, she was already gone." He looked away, and his lower lip trembled. For a moment, Rylie thought he might start to cry. Then he said, "Barbie didn't deserve that. She was beautiful. She was kind. I know what she was trying to do—she was probably trying to stop me from going out and driving drunk. She didn't deserve what I did to her. God, I wish I could take it back."

He paused, his lips moving but no sound coming out, clenching and unclenching his fists, attempting to collect himself. Rylie shuffled in her seat, hoping he wouldn't break down on her. But the next time he spoke, he sounded much stronger, more coherent.

"I've done some things I've regretted. Gambling. Drinking too much. A lot of dumb things. That one tops the list. But unless I'm forgetting—and I could be—I don't think I've done anything that warrants a visit from the Feds. Have I?"

That depended. Maybe he'd done something while blacked out from drinking. Rylie pressed on. "I don't know. You can start off by telling me where you were last night."

"Last night?" He scratched his temple. "I don't know. I guess I started out in one of the watering holes downtown. There are three bars on Main Street. I don't remember which one I went to first. I bounce around. Probably Charlie's, because I like to shoot pool. My friends could probably vouch for me, if I could remember which ones I was with."

That was . . . unhelpful. "And you came home . . . when?"

He shrugged. "After closing? Three. Four? I guess? I don't know. Usually I make it to closing."

"You said these bars are fairly close? So did you drive, or did your friends?"

He shook his head. "Nah. I don't drive anymore."

"You don't?" This wasn't good. "Don't you have a black pick-up truck?"

"Nah."

Before, she'd wondered if he was just being intentionally vague to toy with her, because he didn't like law enforcement. Now, she knew he was outright lying. "I have records on you that say you have a black Dodge R—"

"*Had*." He winced. "Nice truck. Really sweet. But I totaled it last week."

She blinked. "You . . . did? What happened?"

"What do you think happened? I was drunk, and I crashed into someone's house. My truck lost most of its front-end." He gazed at her, quietly assessing her. "I can tell that's not the answer you were looking for, but what can I say? I'm between cars right now."

She eyed him, unsure. Was he lying? Or could his wife's death have screwed him up so badly that he didn't remember kidnapping those girls? Or maybe he'd been drunk? All Rylie knew was that this man was nothing like what she'd expected when he lunged at her with the broken beer bottle. He seemed genuinely remorseful for what he'd done. A shell of a man.

And she hated to admit it, but it sounded like he was telling the truth.

But the last thing she wanted to do was go back to Michael and admit that he was right. She'd nearly gotten herself killed, wasted time . . . all for what?

She knew she was grasping at straws, asking him for help, but she really didn't want this grand idea of hers to be a dead-end.

He went on. "Sorry if I disappointed you, Agent. That's why I thought you were here, for a second. When I realized you weren't a bookie, here for my gambling debts, I thought I was screwed. I thought you were gonna tell me I killed someone else with my driving."

She shook her head. "No. Well, it is about a murder, but it happened outside the town limits."

"I haven't left Sheridan all month. The accident actually happened right around the corner from here." He looked around. "I got a court order, somewhere around here. I got to appear in front of the judge next week so they can dole out my punishment."

She sighed. "Oh. Well, it appears I wasted your time, then."

Rylie began to stand up, but he said, "Why? You said you were here about some murder?"

She shook her head. "It's nothing. You just came up as a suspect for a number of kidnappings we're investigating. The driver has a dark pick-up and has been striking cars on the interstate, forcing young women to have accidents, and then kidnapping them."

"No shit," he said, eyes wide. "And I was a suspect?"

She nodded. "Until now. Though the evidence we had against you was pretty flimsy," she said, though she'd never tell Michael that.

"I guess. So hey . . .." He smiled. "I guess my not having a truck actually was a *good* thing, then. Like my sponsor in AA says, always got to find the bright side."

"You're in AA?"

He laughed. "Occasionally."

He motioned to the door, to see her out. She stepped over the garbage as if she was navigating an obstacle course, and made it safely to the door. "Thank you," she said. "I'm sorry to bother you."

He didn't answer her. As he opened the front door, she looked at him to find his eyes squinted, as if he was deep in thought. He said, "Have you been looking for cars with front-end damage?"

"Yes, but there are so many dark pick-ups in this area that—"

"Well, how many accidents did you say he caused?"

"Three that we know of."

"Three? That has to be some pretty heavy-duty truck, to cause all those accidents without much damage. I bet it's reinforced in the front bumper."

She tilted her head. "Reinforced? What do you mean?"

"Like a grill guard, which is kind of like a cage that people put over their front bumper. It's usually pretty rugged, steel-plated. That thing would bust through anything." He nodded. "Bet you anything he's got one of those."

She took out her phone and opened it. There were three missed calls from her partner. He sure couldn't wait to rub it in her face, could he?

But maybe this trip to interview Buck Finch wasn't a complete waste of time. She opened the browser. "Can you show me what you mean by a cage?"

He took the phone and typed something in on her browser. When the results came up, he handed it back to her. Sure enough, it was as he said—a big, black cage that stretched over the front bumper, transforming it into something of a tank.

"Oh, wow."

"You think your guy might be using one of these?"

"It's a good possibility," she said, pocketing her phone. "Thanks."

"No problem, Agent. Good luck."

She stepped out into the hallway and closed the door. As she did, her phone started to ring again. Of course, it was Michael Brisbane.

She walked down the stairs and out into the alley, lifting the phone to her ear. "What?"

There was a pause. "You can tell me all about Buck when I see you," he said, without a hint of sarcasm in his voice. "But I've been trying to call you because I wanted to let you know . . . another body's been found."

Her heart jammed into her throat. She had to swallow it back in order to speak. "What? When?"

"About half an hour ago. On the side of the highway by milepost 89. From the description, it looks like it's Lila Garrity. I'm on my way there with Lyons. Will you meet us there?"

Her stomach dropped and began to roil again. "Yes. Of course. I'm on my way," she said, reaching her truck.

After she slid into her seat and closed the door, she pounded a fist on the wheel. So what if she'd learned a tiny tidbit about the truck? It seemed so insignificant. People were still dying. And she wasn't any closer to finding out who was responsible.

She started the engine of her truck and headed in the direction of Interstate 86.

## CHAPTER TWENTY FOUR

Twenty minutes later, Rylie arrived at the side of the highway, as she'd done before, to find an ambulance and police cars on the side of the road, and various officials in uniforms and suits standing in a circle, in a field, about fifty yards from the road.

She swallowed the sick feeling in her gut and climbed out of the truck to join them.

She wasn't sure why she felt so bad, now. Deep down, she knew that there was no hope in finding Lila alive. How many of these stories had happy endings? She could count on one hand the number of times someone disappeared with a kidnapper and was found unharmed. So she'd been expecting she would feel terrible.

But right then, her head ached, her bones ached, and more than anything, she was just tired. When she'd gotten into this business, she'd hoped to make a difference and help people from having to endure the nightmare she went through. But she hadn't expected that she'd be reliving that nightmare, day after day, seeing so much evil and spending most days feeling like it was winning.

She'd never felt so beaten.

Michael Brisbane and Jeff Lyons were standing together, making up part of the circle. She trudged toward them and peered between them, at the sight of Lila Garrity. She was clothed, curled into fetal position on her side, looking very much like she was sleeping. But in only a second's glance, Rylie could see the bruising on her throat.

Same as Erin Littlefeather.

She thought about Kiki, her mother, Rose, all lying there, in the dust, motionless. She thought about Maren, screaming as she was hauled away.

It was always the same dance. The evil made their plans and laughed at them as they scurried about like chickens, always one step behind. The detectives in Maren's case had been the same way. She'd cracked her door and watched them, talking to talk her father in the kitchen, saying things like, "There's a possibility" and "In all likelihood, our suspect might . . ."

*Possibilities. Likelihood. Might . . .* all supposition. Never any definite claims.

The detectives and FBI agents came less and less often, but every time they did, they looked more and more beaten. At the time, Rylie hadn't understood. She'd wanted to grab them by the collars of their jackets and scream at them, *Do more! Find her!*

But there was only so much to be done. Sometimes, everything that could be done still wasn't enough.

And crimes would keep on happening, no matter what she did. At that moment, she felt like it'd never end, like it was a hamster wheel of depravity she'd never escape from.

Brisbane caught sight of her and broke from the group, then headed for her. "There's no doubt the murderer in this case is the same as the one that killed that Lakota girl. Everything's pretty much the same."

Rylie didn't look at him. She hugged herself, shivering, and looked out across the plains, toward the Bighorn Mountains. "When was she killed?"

"The medical examiner thinks it was sometime yesterday evening."

"Yesterday evening?" She stiffened. "So that means that this next victim he kidnapped is probably dead unless we find her by tonight."

Brisbane didn't answer, but she knew.

That's what they learned in the academy. *The first 24 hours are crucial in trying to solve a missing persons case.* If she wasn't found today, it was likely all over for college co-ed Ivy Benson.

And then, this would keep going and going. Because what leads did they have? Hardly anything.

After a moment, he said, "What were you saying about Buck's tip about the car?"

She sighed. She knew the question would come up sooner, rather than later, because he probably couldn't resist the opportunity to gloat.

"Nothing," she snapped. "Turns out he smashed up his truck last week and he's far too much of an alcoholic to be our guy. So you were right. I wasted my time going there. Are you happy?"

He looked stricken. She might as well have slapped him across the face. He didn't say anything, just stared at her with a sad look in his eyes.

And she thought it wasn't possible to feel any worse than she had before.

She walked away, into the middle of the field, trying to corral the morbid thoughts whirling in her head.

She only stopped when she reached a massive boulder. She climbed atop it and sat on the smooth surface of it, pulling her knees to her chest and letting the cold wind brace her face.

Maren was the outgoing one. Though it was over twenty years since she'd gone, Rylie still remembered that about her big sister. She was funny, too, the life of the party. She'd dance around and crack jokes and liven the worst of moods. She took after her mom, that way. But Rylie and her dad had been the serious, sedate ones.

With the two live wires of their family gone, no wonder things had fallen apart. Hal had helped hold things together until she'd been able to escape to Seattle for college, but even then, she'd been haunted by the past. By thoughts of Maren. A part of her, the part that kept her from breaking down, wanted her to believe that Maren was still alive. So everywhere she went, every town she passed through, whether it be Quantico, Seattle, or Banner, Wyoming, a little voice inside her brain always asked the question: *Is Maren here? Is she alive, and living in this town?*

But that's what made this case so hard. It was a brutal reminder that kidnappers rarely held onto their victims for long.

Maren was probably long-dead.

She'd dreamed of being a vet. Of working with horses. Of going to see a show on Broadway. Of growing up and studying abroad in Paris. Of having a big family and living on a ranch in the middle of nowhere.

Instead, she probably died, cold and alone, before she reached the age of thirteen.

A tear gathered in the corner of her eye, but she wiped it away before it could escape. The wind. It was just the wind.

She hadn't had one in a long, long time. But right then, more than ever, she could've used a hug from her mother.

# CHAPTER TWENTY FIVE

Ivy Benson woke to total darkness.

At first, she thought she was dead. She could see nothing, feel nothing at all.

But then she heard the gentle thump of the ground beneath her, tires bouncing over rough road, and realized she was in a moving vehicle. A vehicle she couldn't recognize. She dragged her hands around the tight, closed space, feeling nothing but cold metal. Was she in someone's trunk?

It certainly seemed that way. She groped in the darkness, trying to find something to anchor her to the world. The first thing she looked for, of course, was her lifeline. Her cell phone.

But it was gone. She always kept it in the pocket of her jacket, or in her cup holder, when she was driving.

Driving. She'd been driving. That seemed right.

But how had she ended up here, in this dark trunk, being driven God-knows-where? What had happened? The last thing she remembered was getting in her car at Brian's dorm at Casper College, so she could go back to her place at Sheridan. He'd begged her to spend the night, but she'd told him she had to get up early for dance practice.

And then . . . it was a big blur. Try as she might, she couldn't remember anything more than kissing Brian goodnight, ducking into her little car, and pulling away from the curb. He'd called after her to be careful, and she'd driven away, watching him waving at her through her rearview mirror and thinking that he *might* just propose, one day, after graduation.

But after that . . . something had happened. Something terrible. Had she been in an accident?

The second she thought about that possibility, a memory gripped her. A truck, shining its headlights in her window. Trying to intimidate her. But she was never the type to be easily intimidated. She'd once danced an entire show on pointe with a couple of broken toes. She'd given the ass the finger.

Oh, God.

Brian had warned her that her fiery temper was going to get her into trouble one day. Where he was always calm and sedate, she was always doing things like that, inviting trouble. He'd said, *You keep giving the finger to every driver who pisses you off, and one of 'em's gonna pull a gun on you some day.*

Is that what had happened? She squeezed her eyes closed, trying to remember what had happened next.

As she did, the rocking rhythm of the vehicle, jostling her back and forth, began to ease. They were slowing down. Underneath her, the tires screeched to a stop.

She braced herself when she heard the truck's door open, and the sound of heavy footsteps on the ground, moving at a leisurely, yet deliberate pace.

Then, there was a metallic clanking, and suddenly, a door opened up at her side. Light flooded in, and as she blinked away the starbursts in her vision, trying to focus, she realized that she was, indeed, on the bed of a truck.

"Who are you?" she asked at once.

There was no answer.

"There's some mistake," she croaked, her voice cracking from disuse.

"No, I believe there isn't a mistake. I saw you out there, on the road," a rather pleasant male voice said. "And I know you saw me, too."

Slowly, her vision came together. The first thing she made out was a smile. At first, big and beautiful, it made her think everything was all right, that this was just some misunderstanding. But then, the features around the smile solidified. The smile was that of a skeleton—unnaturally wide and sinister. There were thin, barely-there lips that couldn't seem to stretch over the teeth. Around the lips, the skin was so mottled and raw that it looked like the gnarled, twisted bark of an ancient tree. It looked wet and waxy and wrong. Black eyes bulged from their sockets like two golf-balls.

She couldn't fight the scream that erupted from her lips. When he came forward and threw a giant hand over her mouth, the skin of his palms was rough and waxy, too.

"Don't do that," he said, his voice still pleasant.

*Calm, Ivy. You have to be calm. Use your head. Maybe you can reason with him.*

After a moment, he removed his hand, and she took a deep breath. "What happened?"

"To me? Someone like *you.*" He spat the word with hatred.

She wasn't sure what that meant. All she knew was that she was on this man's bad side. For what, she couldn't know. "Did I do something wrong?"

"You don't remember engaging with me on the highway last night?" he asked, one of his non-existent eyebrows quirking up. He didn't have much hair, either, just a few dark patches, here and there, on his head. Had he been burned? She wasn't a medical expert, but that was what it looked like.

But she only looked for a moment, because the sight was so horrifying, it made nausea bubble in her gut. She closed her eyes and said, "Engaging?"

"Yes. Rude gestures?"

More of it came to her, the sight of the headlights, in her back window. The way he rode her bumper, like he was trying to get her to react. She could've argued, telling him that he was the instigator, but she didn't want to anger him. So instead, she said, "I'm sorry, I shouldn't have done that. I apologize."

"You do?" He tilted his head.

"Yes. Absolutely. I'm sorry. Please. Don't hurt me. If you let me go, I won't tell anyone."

He chuckled, as sound wet and phlegmy. "Oh, darling, believe me, I count on you not telling anyone, anyway."

Those words hit her like a thunderbolt. "Wh—what do you mean? What are you going to do with me?"

The smile was already sickly wide, but it seemed to crack open even more, revealing blood-red gums. His dark eyes twinkled. "You'll see. But not yet. I promised that I would take my time with you, and I plan to make good on that."

## CHAPTER TWENTY SIX

When they returned to the police station, Rylie got out of her truck and trudged toward the door. She didn't want to go in. The walls of that little room had been closing in on her before, and now, she felt like they'd suffocate her.

"Hey . . . you forget something?" a voice said, stirring her from her thoughts.

She looked up to see Michael. He'd ridden back to the police station with Officer Lyons, and he hadn't spoken to her at all since she returned from her walk out into the field. She could tell from the look in his eyes—he thought she was crazy. Here he was, a person who could have a conversation with a wall, and he was speechless around her.

She shook her head. "I'm fine."

He gave her a doubtful look, a look she was so accustomed to receiving. It was one that said, *What the hell is wrong with you?*

The answer, she didn't want to tell.

She'd effectively boxed him out, just like she did to every person she ran across. She'd had a couple friends in Seattle—Jim, her boyfriend of five years. Cooper Rich, a fellow agent. A few other people she spoke to. But she always kept all of them at arm's distance, never fully letting any of them in. She didn't want to be vulnerable to anyone. And so, whenever her PTSD came out and she acted like a lunatic, they treated her like one—they turned their backs on her. No one understood why she was the way she was.

Well, one person did.

She stopped halfway up the stairs, as Brisbane held the door open for her. Then she took a step down. "You know what? I forgot. I need to make a phone call. I'll be right back."

He simply shrugged and continued inside.

She wandered around to the old bench, on the side of the police station, sat down, and dialed Hal's number.

"Hey, baby girl," he said without missing a beat. "You calling to tell me you're in the area and paying me a visit?"

She smiled, like she always did when she heard his voice. "No. Sorry. Not yet."

"Damn. I've got some fine barbecue on the grill right now. You'd love it."

She licked her lips, remembering the taste of his barbecue ribs. There wasn't anything like it in the world. It was probably the only thing that could get her appetite going. "I'd love it," she said, "But I'll have to take a raincheck."

He clucked his tongue in disappointment. "What's got you so down, now?"

She laughed. It wasn't like she was standing in front of him. And yet he always seemed to know whenever she was in a mood. "Nothing!"

"Don't give me that. Is this about your daddy?"

"No." At least Hal didn't have a completely open window to her soul. "It's not. I mean, yes . . . last night, I thought about calling him. But I didn't."

"Now why'd you think about doing that? Last time I spoke to you, you said if he wanted to get in touch with you, he had your number."

"Right. But the more I thought about it, the more I wondered . . . I don't know . . . my mom would've wanted me to reach out. To repair things." She sighed, "But you know my dad isn't the most talkative person on earth. He'd probably be dying to get me off the phone."

"You don't know that. He might surprise you."

She leaned back on the bench and looked up at the blue sky. "Maybe. But I don't really have time for that now. I'm investigating a case. Kidnapping and murders of young females."

"Ah. How's it going?"

"Over like a lead balloon," she said with a bitter laugh. "Not well. We just found the second victim and I think tonight, there might be a third."

"No wonder you're thinking back to me, to the old days," he said, his voice full of sympathy. "That cuts a little close to home, don't it?"

"Yeah," she said, laughing again because otherwise she was afraid she'd cry. "But I'm coping."

"Not too well, from the sound of it, girl. Are you sure you're okay?"

"Yeah. I'm—" This time, her voice cracked. "Just tired. No sleep."

"Well, girl. You might not be able to help Maren right now. But you do have the potential to help people. What you couldn't do with

Maren has no bearing on what you *can* do with this case. And I think you're going to give this cretin hell. Hog-tie him and send him straight back to hell." He bit off the last words with energy; for an old guy, he sure was feisty.

"Well, I'll try."

"You'll *do*." He said it with such confidence, Rylie felt a burst of longing for him. She wanted to go and visit him, as soon as she could. "There ain't nothing you set out to do that you don't accomplish, baby girl. You go get 'em."

"Thanks."

She ended the call and sat there, on the bench, staring up the sky. Two eagles circled overhead, making arcs and figure eights across the sky. She closed her eyes and tried to channel that person Hal Buxton thought she was—calm, collected, capable of accomplishing anything.

Suddenly, the answer came to her. It was one she'd been in the midst of forming, when she got the terrible news about Lila's body being found.

She marched into the station. When she came to the cramped break room, she found it almost a carbon copy of what it was, before Lila Garrity's body was found—the team was still poring over files and looking for leads but finding nothing. Michael Brisbane was leaning over the computer, listening with mild disgust to Beeker's theory, which involved lizard people.

"It's possible. The more I read into this underground stuff, the more I start to believe it," he said with a shrug.

"Dude," Brisbane said, pointing to the computer. "Stick to real facts, and things you don't just read on the internet, okay? Stay out of the dark web and stick to your Star Wars marathons. Got it?"

Beeker shrugged and unwrapped a lollypop. "Okay. I'm just—"

"And brush your teeth every once in a while, okay? You smell like Doritos." He ruffled his hair.

The two agents had worked together before Rylie had joined them. Rylie had to admit, it was kind of sweet to see the way that Michael had taken the kid under his wing. He was always giving him tips when they were together, like a big brother. Rylie didn't know much about the kid—she made it a point not to get too close to anyone—but he had to be a little lost, working out of the new field office, away from his friends and family.

"We've gone through all the names on the list Beeker provided," Brisbane said to her when she came in, pounding a fist on the table in frustration. "And they've gotten us nowhere."

"That's because I don't think his pick-up is black," Rylie said, her voice strong and authoritative. "In fact, I'm pretty sure it's not."

"What do you mean, it's not? Of course it is," Beeker said, not looking up from his computer. He was sucking on a lollypop, still crisscross-applesauce on the floor, despite there being an open chair for him. He hadn't moved at all since this morning.

"Uh, yeah, Wolf, what else could it be?" Brisbane said gently, pointing to the file. "Remember? We have black paint detected on each of the women's cars, and—"

"But what if it wasn't the truck that hit them?" Rylie said.

His face twisted in confusion. "Uh . . . what does that mean? What else could've hit them?"

"What if the truck was reinforced in the front with a black steel cage to withstand the impact, and *that's* what's been leaving black paint on the cars?"

Beeker finally glanced up, his mouth opening slightly, lollypop forgotten. It fell out of his mouth and landed on his crotch. "Wait. You mean . . . like a tank?"

Brisbane shook his head. "Like a cage, right? Yeah, I never thought about that. My uncle had one of those." He snapped his fingers. "I bet we could look into places in the area that sell and install those. There can't be very many of them. Beeker--"

"Already on it," Beeker said, picking up his lollypop, stuffing it back in his mouth and continuing to type.

Brisbane smiled at her. "Smart thinking, Agent. Where did that idea come from?"

"I don't know—it might be just another wild goose chase. But the idea was supplied to me by Buck Finch."

"Ah. So it was a worthwhile trip after all."

She shrugged. "We'll see if it brings any results."

"Okay, guys," Beeker spoke up, clapping his hands. "I got only one place in all of Sheridan County that installs those cages and steel reinforcements. Website's a hot mess. Who uses Wix anymore for their business?"

Rylie looked. From first glance, it wasn't very professional, with oddly-shaped graphics and difficult-to-read copy.

Beeker continued to read. "Geez, from this map, it looks like it's out in the middle of nowhere. They do custom jobs for locals." He stopped and whistled. "Whoa. And look at his."

He turned the computer toward them to give them a better look at the photograph of a red truck, its entire front grill fitted with a thick black cage.

"Sweet set-up, huh? Bet a lot of you country boys from around here like this shit, huh, Bris?"

Brisbane shrugged. "Never owned a pick-up in my life. But that looks good. They have a phone number?"

"Right here." Beeker pointed to the screen.

Brisbane picked up his phone and dialed the number. Rylie waited, feeling antsy as he listened, then rolled his eyes and ended the call. "Damn. Number's out of service."

"It closed down?" Beeker scrolled through the website. "Doesn't say it's closed down. Says it's open until five today. Michael Sabado, Proprietor."

Rylie checked the time on the clock over the coffee station. It was just after two.

"We should probably go out there and check around," Rylie said, standing up, feeling more energized than she had all day. She took a step for the door and gave her partner a curious look. "Unless you think it'd be a waste of time?"

He rolled his eyes. "It might be, but fine. I guess we have nothing better to do." He looked at Beeker. "Where is it?"

Beeker scribbled the address on a piece of paper and handed it to them. "May the force be with you."

# CHAPTER TWENTY SEVEN

As they drove into the foothills of the Bighorn Mountains, Rylie noted Michael Brisbane was back to his old self. He was eating from a bag of M&Ms, chewing noisily. When he offered her some, and she declined, he said, "Are you feeling better?"

She glanced over at him as she checked the GPS and took a right onto an unpaved road that cut through an oil field. "What are you talking about? I wasn't feeling bad, at all. Geez, this place is out in the middle of nowhere."

He looked around and nodded. "You looked like you were pissed that I didn't agree with you about going out to Finch's."

"I wasn't pissed. You're your own person. You can do whatever you want to do."

He tossed back his head and emptied the last of the candies into his mouth, then crushed the bag. "Not really. As partners, we're kind of supposed to come to a consensus. Back each other up."

"Well . . . you didn't agree with me. So I had to go off on my own. Nearly got stabbed in the throat with a broken bottle, too."

He stared at her, looking for the punch line. When she didn't give it to him, he said, "You're serious?"

"Yep. He was drunk and he flew into a rage."

"Wow. Shit. You're making friends all over the place," he said, shaking his head. "And you know, that's the thing. That's what I'm trying to say, but not doing too good a job of it. I was supposed to back you up. Go with you. And I didn't. And I'm sorry, Wolf. Really. It won't happen again."

She glanced over at him. He looked so earnest, and legitimately upset with himself.

"Hey. You were right, though. Finch *was* a dead end. The info about the cage was really just dumb luck. So don't feel too bad."

He nodded. "Okay. Fair enough. But I just want you to know—it was out of line for me to shut your idea down like that."

"Well, I pretty much shut you down, too."

He chuckled. “All right. We’ve established we suck at cooperation. Honestly, though? I would’ve gone with you. I was just in a bad mood.”

“You? I didn’t know you got in those.”

He nodded and looked straight ahead, and the next time he spoke, all humor was gone from his voice. “I think it goes along with the job. I don’t think any one of us would’ve gotten into this line of business if we didn’t have something personal invested in it.”

She glanced over at him, hoping he’d expand on that. But he didn’t. She wanted to ask him what he meant, but she knew that if she did, she’d have to tell him her own secrets. And she couldn’t do that.

Besides, they could still cooperate without knowing every little thing about one another. They were partners, not lovers.

So she decided to change the subject and leave that one behind. “This place sure is creepy,” she said as they bounced over the rutted road.

“Tell me about it.”

It had been lovely, while they were driving toward the mountains, with the sun just about to dip behind them in the cloudless, light blue sky. But now that they were in the shadow of the giant hills, the dusty, vacant fields, with only a few abandoned shacks and miles overgrown with scrubby brush, seemed eerie and foreboding. It gave off ghost town vibes, like the start of some horror movie.

“I can’t believe that any business can be all the way out here, in the middle of nowhere,” he said. “If they closed down, no wonder. No one can find this place. I wonder if Beeker gave us the right address. He can be a knucklehead.”

“I’m sure it’s the right address,” she said, checking the GPS. “It says it’s right up here around this hill.”

As she said that, they passed a sign that said, WARNING: MANY VISITORS HAVE BEEN GORED BY BUFFALO.

Brisbane laughed. “You see any buffalo around here?”

“That’s a National Park Service sign,” she said. “And this isn’t a national park. Someone must’ve stolen it.”

A few seconds later, they passed a sign, hand-painted and faded from the sun, that said, KEEP OUT EXCEPT ON OFFICIAL BUZNESS.

This time, Rylie had to laugh. Especially when they passed a fence made entirely out of barbed wire. Then another one. It felt like they were venturing into a camp for prison inmates. Rylie kept her eyes on the dirt road ahead of her, wondering if the next thing they were going to come across were mines, or men with machine guns.

"I don't know why this guy didn't get more business. The atmosphere's so welcoming," Brisbane muttered as they came to a litany of signs—*NO TRESPASSING. KEEP OUT. NO SOLLICITING. VIOLATORS WILL BE SHOT ON SITE. SURVIVORS WILL BE SHOT AGAIN! GO AWAY. THIS IS YOUR LAST WARNING. GUS'S ARMORY 1 MILE AHEAD.*

"Is this guy insane, or what?" Rylie mumbled, slowing down to read the signs.

Brisbane held up a finger. "Wait. I get it. You know what he is? He's one of those . . . what are they called . . . .." he said, searching for the word. "You know. A Doomsday Prepper."

"You think?"

He nodded. "Yeah. I had an uncle who lived upstate who did the same thing. He has a metal bunker underground filled with everything he needs to survive the next apocalypse. He had enough freeze-dried food down there to last him for years."

"That probably means I'll be the first victim of the apocalypse. I never even have enough food in my apartment for the next day, much less the next several years," she said, squinting as the dust from the road puffed up into her line of vision. "But what does that have to do with creating reinforcements for trucks?"

"Don't you get it?" he said, as if the answer was obvious. "When the bombs fall, there will be a lot of wreckage everywhere. Everything will be destroyed. So people will need a tough, tank-like truck to get them through and take them from place to place."

"Oh. Really? I never thought of that."

He shrugged. "Or something. I never really listened to my uncle's rantings. He was a little crazy."

When they came around the corner, there was no doubt that the man who lived there was crazy. Probably *a lot* crazy, from the appearance of Gus's Armory. The front fence was covered with all kinds of hub caps, and there were all types of antennas, sprouting from the roof of the shack. It looked like a crude space station. A dusty sign among the refuse said, *Welcome to Gus's Armory—Custom Steel Fittings for your Vehicle.*

Well, that was slightly friendly.

The fence was open, too, so they pulled into the yard. The doors and windows of the small shack were closed, the shades pulled tight.

The roof was corrugated metal, mostly rusted. There was a sign on the front door, dangling askew from a single nail, that said, *OUT TO LUNCH—FOREVER!* So maybe it was closed? But in the yard, she noticed several trucks, all with massive black cages over their front grills. There was a small garage with two open bays, and a rather impressive workbench with tools and fittings.

"Doesn't look like anyone is here. But those vehicles look newly washed, don't they?" Rylie said. "We should check them all out for any damage."

"My thoughts exactly," he said, pulling off his seatbelt and getting out of the truck as she did the same.

They both hurried to the closest truck and stooped to inspect it. The truck was old and rusted, and the cage was full of more than its share of dents and scuffs.

"Hell. This truck looks like its former owners were a couple of crash test dummies," Brisbane remarked, going around the side and peering in the window. It was open, so he stuck his head inside. "What do you think? Could be our vehicle, huh?"

"It's possible," she said, walking over to the next one. That one, too, had numerous dents and dings. "It could be this one?"

Brisbane looked around the lot. "Could be any of these damn trucks. They all look like they've been through more than a few accidents. What the hell does this guy do?"

Rylie opened her mouth to answer, but she was interrupted by the sound of a gun, being cocked. "Can't you read? No trespassing," a low voice growled.

They turned in unison to find themselves staring down a double-barrel shotgun. The man was standing on his porch, right outside his front door.

Rylie's instincts took over. She reached underneath her jacket and pulled her gun from its holster, leveling it at once. "FBI. Drop it."

The slight, bald man, with a gray beard and overalls, didn't even falter. He squeezed one eye closed and aimed his gun right at Rylie.

Brisbane just raised his hands. "Whoa, whoa, guys. I think there's some misunderstanding."

"Ain't no misunderstanding," the man said. "I had signs up all over the place. No trespassing. And you ignored 'em. I don't care what badge you're holding. This is private property. And no government agency's gonna disrespect me on that. You hear?"

"We don't want any trouble. We just had some questions," Brisbane continued, motioning for Rylie to stand down. "About an investigation we're conducting."

"I'm sure you do. But listen to me. I don't know nothin'. I stay out of other people's business. And I expect people to do me the same courtesy. So I can't help you. Got that?"

Rylie kept her gun level. "Drop your weapon. We'll bring you in by force, if we have to."

"Over my dead body, girlie," he said, and for a moment she thought he might pull the trigger. She squeezed her own finger on her trigger, dangerously close to firing. She couldn't let him get away. Not now, after all this.

But suddenly, the man lowered his gun. "I still ain't helping. I can't. I don't know nothing."

She looked at Brisbane. "If he's not going to cooperate . . . we have to bring him in."

"Gus . . . is that your name?" he said, walking slowly toward the man.

The suspicion on his doughy, red face didn't subside. "Yeah."

Rylie lowered her gun.

Michael spoke pleasantly. "I think you might know more than you think. And I understand you wanting to keep out of others' business. But there's been some murders."

He shook his head. "Murders? Around here? And I suppose you think I got somethin' to do with it. Well I got news for you. I ain't left this place all year. I don't need to. I don't need nothin' outside that fence."

"No," Rylie said. "You're not a suspect. We just want to talk."

His eyes narrowed in confusion. "What can I possibly tell you? I haven't seen nothin'. Like I said. I ain't left this place."

"But you have had customers who've gotten modifications on their cars, yes?" Brisbane asked. "That's what you do here, right?"

"Well, yeah. But . . ."

"That's what we're looking for. We have reason to believe that our killer might have a truck that was outfitted with these special modifications."

Gus's eyes widened, and he looked away. "Yeah? Well I got nothing to do with those murders. Like I said, I've been here. I ain't done nothin' wrong."

"We're not saying that you did. But if you come down to the precinct with us, maybe we can—"

"No." He stiffened. "I can't help you. I ain't goin' nowhere."

"Look," Rylie said, pleading, "So far, he's killed two young, innocent girls, and kidnapped a third. And if we don't get some answers soon, that girl might die tonight."

His jaw opened, hanging slack. His eyes went from Michael, to Rylie, then back to Michael again. "Wait. Young . . . girls?" His voice was small.

Brisbane nodded.

"All right. You said he had a modified truck? What do you want to know?"

Rylie motioned to her truck. "Why don't you come downtown to the police with us so we can speak to you on record?"

He sighed. "All right. Fine."

Brisbane looked at Rylie, surprise evident on his face. She felt it, too. There was something odd about this. After all that commotion, he'd agreed to accompany them almost too easily.

So what were they missing?

# CHAPTER TWENTY EIGHT

Thirty minutes later, Rylie stood in the small conference room at the police station with Michael Brisbane, her arms folded over her chest as they interrogated the old man.

She really didn't know about this one. Sure, he had trucks that looked like they'd been through the ringer. He was a misanthrope, with a bit of a weird, aggressive personality, considering how quick he'd been to pull that gun. And he'd been acting rather squirrely—going from ready to run them off his homestead to willingly accompanying them down to the police station in a matter of moments? Something was off about him. He was hiding something.

Brisbane seemed ready to snap the cuffs on him, but there were other things that gave Rylie pause. She'd pulled a report on Gus Mason, finding very little. He'd served in Vietnam as a teenager, had no rap sheet at all, not even a speeding ticket. He'd pretty much lived off-the-grid, ever since he'd returned home from the war. For him to suddenly start going around, murdering women? It just didn't seem right.

So maybe that's why she let her partner take the lead. He clearly seemed to think they were onto something, based on his line of questioning.

"What kind of modifications did you do for your clients?" Brisbane asked, his voice uncharacteristically hard-edged.

"Like you said, front grill covers . . .armored sides . . . things like that."

Rylie pulled out her phone and navigated to his website. There were a number of pictures of completed jobs, done by Gus's outfit.

Brisbane said, "How many jobs do you do in a given month?"

He laughed. "I only do about three or four a year."

"You employ anyone else?"

He shook his head.

"You live with anyone else?"

"No. It's just me."

"Do you have a list of, or do you remember the clients that you've worked with?"

He nodded. "I personally know every one of my clients. They're all friends of mine."

"So none of them have ever struck you as suspicious?"

He chuckled. "I'm suspicious of everyone. Even my friends."

"Have you helped repair any damage to any front grills in the past?"

He shook his head. "Nah. I don't do that. If one's broken, it's easier to just outfit it with a whole new cage."

"Have you done that for anyone in the past year?"

"Nope. Not recently."

Michael looked at her, and she could tell he was a little exasperated, not getting the information he wanted. She knew that with his next line of questioning, he'd go for the jugular, and she was right.

"You seemed a little nervous back there, when we mentioned the murders," Brisbane said, shoving his hands into his pockets. "You mind telling me what that was all about?"

He shrugged. "Wasn't nervous."

Rylie continued to scroll through the website, when she came across something very interesting about other modifications that could be done to cars, beyond reinforced cages. Secret compartments, under seats, in various other locations as well.

Suddenly, something came to her. She navigated to another website, only half-listening to the questioning, her fingers flying over the keyboard. If her suspicions were correct . . .

She came to the article and started reading as Brisbane said, "Agent Wolf and I would beg to differ."

*MURDERED MAN HAD $120K OF METH IN SECRET COMPARTMENT IN HIS CAR*

*ARVADA—After two men were found murdered on the side of I-86 last week, more than $120,000 worth of methamphetamine was found in a secret compartment in the car.*

*Investigators found the drugs in the car after being called to the scene, months after narcotics and intelligence agents first became aware of Luis Hernandez and Jose Valdez. They found both Hernandez and Valdez, shot in the head.*

*Federal authorities had notified local agents that the pair was believed to be involved in high-level cocaine and meth transportation and distribution. Local officials spent months tracking them.*

*After the murders were committed, a police dog at the scene alerted that something was in the vehicle, and agents searched it. Police found a trap between the back seats and the trunk of the car that held more than 15 pounds of meth in "various stages of production." Investigators said it had a street value of more than $120,000.*

"Had nothing to do with nothing," she heard Gus say, and looked up.

Gus looked away and drummed his slim fingers on the table.

"Did it have something to do with the Arvada murders?" Rylie suddenly blurted.

"What?" Brisbane and Gus said in unison.

"The Arvada murders," she said, showing the article to him. "Was one of your 'special enhancements' creating secret compartments in cars?"

Gus started to choke. "Water. I need water."

She rolled her eyes. "Was it?"

As benevolent as he was, Brisbane rushed out the door to get him his water. She leaned forward and waited for the answer as he caught his breath.

"Are you going to answer me?"

He gazed at her like a puppy, caught peeing in the wrong place. Brisbane returned with the glass, just as Gus said, meekly, "Well . . . yeah."

Brisbane set the glass down, shaking his head in disappointment. "That's what you thought this was about? *Those* murders?"

He sucked down half the glass before speaking. "Yeah. But then you said it was about some girls."

"It is. These girls have been hunted down by a man who we believe has a reinforced truck, similar to the ones you own. This male—who the victims have described as creepy—obviously has something against these women."

"I don't got nothin' against nobody. So I'm clean. Nothin' to hide." He shrugged. "And it ain't illegal to build those compartments in a car. In this state, anyway."

"But you know hidden compartments aren't used for anything good," Brisbane said, straightening. "You knew those two guys?"

"Nah. Not well. And I don't know who killed 'em, either."

"That doesn't matter," Rylie said, looking at Brisbane to continue. "That's not what you're here for."

"Right." Brisbane said, crossing his arms over his chest. "Like we said, you do have trucks on your property that could've been responsible for the accidents that occurred before the kidnapping. The fronts of them are awfully banged up."

"Yeah. It's dark out here. Lot of critters. I used to hit deer all the time when I drove, but never fixed them up afterwards. That's all."

"You loan your cars out to anyone?"

He shook his head. "And like I said, I ain't gone anywhere, either."

"But you don't have anyone who can confirm that, since you live alone. Right?"

His face drained of color. "Well . . . no. But you ain't sayin' I'm responsible for those girls? I don't know nothin' about this!"

"So you'll let us search your place?" Brisbane fired back.

He shrugged. "I ain't killed no girls. If it'll clear me from whatever other crime you think I committed."

Rylie watched him, then whispered in Brisbane's ear. "Can I talk to you for a moment, outside, Agent?"

He nodded and followed her out. Before she'd even closed the door, he said, "I think he's lying."

She blinked in surprise. "What makes you say that? I was about to tell you I don't think we have nearly enough to keep him."

"Yeah, but—"

"You saw his profile. It's clean. He's a loner. And he makes a few bucks putting secret compartments in cars, yes. But I don't think he's a killer."

"But those trucks, Wolf. And you saw it, too. He wanted to get us away from his place. That's why he agreed so easily to come to the station. He was trying to lead us away from the evidence."

She shook her head and said nothing.

"We should at least have the trucks analyzed. Conduct a search of the property and see if we can find anything."

"Ivy?"

He nodded. "Yeah. Maybe she's there."

"But if she is, why would he let us search his place?"

He shrugged. "I don't know. Maybe he's got her so hidden away in one of his secret compartments in his place, he doesn't think we'll find her. He's got a few screws loose. Maybe he's just playing games. Maybe he kidnapped her, but she isn't there. We should at least check."

He motioned to Officer Lyons and said, "Have Gus brought to a holding area for now. Let's get a couple guys together to go down to Gus's Armory and check it out, all right?"

"Yes, sir," Lyons said with great enthusiasm, heading off to gather his team.

Rylie hesitated as he began to walk away. He stopped. "What? You have problems with that?"

"No . . . it makes sense. It's better to be safe. Especially if Ivy might be there. But . . ."

"But what?" He stooped a little to look into her eyes.

"Well . . . I know we just talked about backing each other up and everything . . . but do you mind if I hang back here and look into some things?"

"What things?" He raised an eyebrow. "You have a hunch on something?"

"Yeah. It was just something you said. About the guy having something against the young women he kidnaps. That makes sense. He doesn't sexually assault them. He wants them for something else. And why else would you keep anyone in your possession for a few hours, only to kill them? The only thing I can think of is revenge."

"For what?"

"Well, that's the question. Maybe a young woman did something to him in the past. So maybe I should be looking into crimes around this area where a young woman was the perpetrator. You know, just in case your search doesn't turn up anything. What do you think?"

He nodded. "That does make sense. You want to stay here with Beeker while I check things out?"

She smiled. "Well, we just got done agreeing we'd back each other up. If we separate . . ."

"If I go with the police officers, and you're here with Beeker, I think we'll both have backup. But this way, we can cover more ground."

"You should be careful, though," she said to him. "A place like that, for a man like Gus? I wouldn't put it past him to have booby traps and hidden doors and all sorts of crazy things."

"Yeah. I thought about that. We will." He held up his phone. "Just text me if you find anything."

"As long as you do the same for me," she said.

He gave her a thumbs-up. "It's a deal."

# CHAPTER TWENTY NINE

It was near dark by the time the party set out from the station to search Gus's Armory. Rylie stayed in the break room, sucking down coffee and sitting with Beeker as he went through the computer, compiling the files that she was looking for.

"How far do you want me to go back, boss?" he asked, typing so fast, his hands were a blur over the keys.

"Twenty years? Can you go back that far?"

"Of course. We're the FBI. We can do anything," he said with a grin. He pressed enter. "And there. Now it'll just take a couple minutes, and we'll have our results."

"Great."

She picked up her phone and texted Brisbane: *Find anything yet?*

A moment later, he responded: *We haven't even gotten there yet. Antsy, aren't you?*

She was. She would've gone with him, though, if she'd thought that his search was going to yield anything. But she had a distinct feeling that it would be a bust. That, just like Brisbane had felt about Buck Finch, it would be a wild goose chase.

No, she'd been thinking more and more about it, in the moments since he left. Now, she closed her eyes, and pretended she was on the side of the road, watching and waiting for a young girl to pass by.

He didn't know them. He only knew them by sight. He went out, like a man on a hunting expedition, especially looking for young women.

Once he found one, he made the split-second decision to follow her. He'd follow her, so she'd be creeped out. He'd maybe play cat-and-mouse with her, taunting her.

And then he'd strike. But not hard. He wanted his victims alive.

Why?

*Revenge.* That word kept popping into Rylie's mind.

But for what?

An answer came to her, almost immediately.

*For someone doing the same thing to him.*

Her eyes flew open. Beeker had stood up and was now standing in front of the vending machine, pressing the button for a Coke.

"Beeker," she said, her heart thudding heavily in her chest. "Can you narrow that list down to car accidents on the I-86 corridor, over the past twenty years, with a young woman, ages 18 to 29, and a man involved, and where someone in the man's party was killed?"

He nodded. "I think I can do that."

He went back to his computer and typed some more. She stood up and started to pace.

A moment later, he said, "All right, all right. I've got a few hits, here in Sheridan county. This one, a big crash with a semi. Everyone died."

She stopped pacing and shook her head. "No . . . not that one. What else?"

"This one . . . two muscle cars were drag racing after hours and a nineteen-year-old who was a passenger in one of the cars died when the driver lost control."

"No . . . that's not right, either. You have anything else?"

"Just one more . . .." he said, clicking on it. "This one was about fifteen years ago. A road rage case between a twenty-three-year-old nursing student and a forty-eight-year-old man. The man lost control of his car and drove into a tree. He was killed instantly. The woman survived." He scrolled down some more. "His son was in the car. He was severely injured."

Rylie froze. Then she walked over and peered over his shoulder at the report. The boy, Cameron Wakely, was air-lifted to the hospital in Laramie with burns over ninety percent of his body. She noticed a couple of articles attached to the report. "Can you click on that one?"

"Sure thing." He brought up an article with a photograph of a burned-out shell of a pick-up truck, with officials standing around it. "Whoa."

She nudged him out of the way and started to read:

*BELOVED FOOTBALL COACH KILLED IN ROAD RAGE INCIDENT*

*SHERIDAN- A youth football coach was killed and his son was wounded in a road rage highway incident on I-86 on Tuesday night outside of Sheridan.*

*Jason Wakely was fatally hit while driving his son home after coaching a game, police said.*

*Jason's son was in the car with him, when it is believed another vehicle cut them off. It is believed that the other driver had some kind of altercation on the road that led to a high-speed chase, resulting in Wakely losing control of the car and leaving the road before crashing into a tree and sparking an enormous fire.*

*The father was transported to Laramie Medical Center and pronounced dead. Wakely's son survived the crash but is in critical condition at Laramie Medical Center.*

*Sheridan police believe the other driver was driving a light-colored Ford Mustang or possibly a Dodge Charger. Chief of Police Eric Rumford confirmed that responding officers "determined that the driver of the vehicle had been killed on impact" and that he died as a result of what "may have been some sort of traffic altercation between the two drivers."*

*One witness at the nearby exit recalled hearing the collision after Wakely's car smashed into the tree.*

*"I heard a very loud crash, very loud crash," a resident of the apartment complex, who gave only her first name, Michelle said. "When I heard it was Jason, I was dumbstruck. He coached my son in little stars football. He will be greatly missed. By a lot of people."*

She scanned the rest of the article, then motioned to the link for the other article. "It said that a young woman was responsible for the altercation?"

"Yeah . . . I think. I guess she left the scene of the crime and was picked up later." He clicked on the link.

*SHERIDAN WOMAN CLEARED IN MANSLAUGHTER CHARGE IN ALLEGED ROAD RAGE INCIDENT*

*Youth football coach Jason Wakely, 42, was killed Tuesday in a car crash that resulted from a roadside dispute, Sheridan police say. The suspected instigator, Valerie Hopkins, 22, was charged with manslaughter, but those charges were dropped late yesterday.*

*Hopkins fled after the deadly encounter. She was later arrested on a charge of manslaughter, police said.*

*"Our original investigation revealed Wakely, the driver of a truck, was engaged in an altercation with Hopkins, driving a car," police said. "But there is no reason to believe that Hopkins instigated or was directly responsible for the driver's loss of control."*

*Wakely was pronounced dead at the hospital, police said.*

"Valerie Hopkins," Rylie murmured. "Can you look her up and tell me what happened to her?"

"Yep. One sec." He typed a little bit more, and second later, whistled. "Dead. One year ago."

"Dead? What happened?"

He shrugged as he squinted at the screen. "Oh. Wow. Looks like she was murdered by an intruder who was never found."

Rylie's pulse pounded in her throat. "And how long ago did all this happen?"

"The road rage incident? Fifteen years ago."

"So the little boy . . . Cameron. How old would he be, now, do you think?"

He stared at the screen for a moment. "Uh . . . he was twelve then, so mid-thirties?"

"Do you have any information about him?"

Beeker laughed. "What did I tell you? We are the FBI. We have information about *everyone*." He typed a little bit, and froze. "Oh. That's interesting."

She straightened. "What?"

"We don't have any information about a Cameron Wakely in Wyoming."

"There's nothing?"

"No, that can't be right. Hold on." He typed some more and frowned. "Well, hell."

She stooped to look at the screen. "What does that mean? Tell me."

"Well . . . the last article I have on him was from two years after the accident. And then . . . nothing. It's like he's a phantom."

"You're joking."

"I don't ever joke." He smirked.

She motioned to the screen. "Bring up that article. The last one."

He did, and she scanned it. *SHERIDAN COMMUNITY RALLIES AROUND INJURED BOY.* There was no photograph, but she read the article with growing interest. Apparently, his burns were so extensive, he was flown to a burn center in Denver. He didn't have enough healthy skin for skin grafts, so they had to grow skin for him. So far, he'd had at least a dozen surgeries, with many more likely.

"Oh, that poor kid," she said, shaking her head. "But what could've happened to him?"

Beeker shrugged. "Must've gone off-the-grid."

"But the FBI can get info on anyone."

"Maybe not. Millions of people in this country. Guess some can fall through the cracks. Weirder things have happened."

She shrugged into her jacket and motioned to the computer. "Can you give me the address? The last known place the Wakelys lived?"

He scribbled it down and went to hand it to her, but suddenly yanked it away. "Hey. Wait. You're not going to go there?"

"Yeah. Might as well check it out. Why not?"

Beeker frowned. "*Why not?* Because Bris told me to keep an eye on you."

She laughed, a little confused. "What? Why does he think I need a babysitter? Especially one who isn't even old enough to drink legally?"

"Hey," he raised his palms. "First of all, I'm twenty-two. Secondly, he didn't do it out of spite or anything. Mike's a good guy. He did it because he would hate if anything happened to you."

"I know, I know," she groaned. "Because we're partners and he'd feel responsible."

He shook his head. "No. Because he cares about you."

She blinked. She hadn't heard anyone say that out loud about her, in so long. "What?"

"And I know you care about him. Even if you don't say it."

Her eyes narrowed. "How did you—"

"Because it's as impossible not to care about him as it is for him not to care about others. He's a big softie. You can't not like him. And you guys are partners. Maybe only for a couple weeks, but that bond is strong. Or at least, that's what he tells me." He shrugged, "That's what he said about his last partner, anyway."

"Oh," she said, feeling completely out of her element. "Well, I wouldn't know. He's my first partner. I'm not used to—"

"Well, I don't think he'd want you going out there, alone, at night."

She hesitated. Funny, if this was Seattle, she'd have already been in her truck, headed to this guy's old house. But she'd made a promise to Brisbane. "You could come with me?"

Beeker shook his head. "Unfortunately, while you guys are my favorite agents in the office, you're not the only ones I'm doing work for, boss. I've got a shitload of case files to get to."

"Oh." Well, she'd only promised her partner that she'd tell him what she found. So she would. "I'll be back soon. Probably well before Bris gets back."

"Wolf, you know that Bris is gonna have my hide for this."

"Well, tell him too bad. I'm my own woman and I appreciate his concern, but he's not my keeper. Besides, the guy was last there fifteen years ago. I'm sure he's long gone. I just wouldn't feel like I was doing a thorough job unless I checked it out."

He shrugged and gave her a look that said, *Your funeral.*

Then she went out to her truck and, sitting in the front seat, typed in a text to Michael Brisbane: *I got a lead for a Cameron Wakely in Sheridan. It might turn out to be nothing, I'm going to check it out.*

She stared at it for a moment, daring him to tell her it was a bad idea.

But there was no response. It showed on her phone as delivered, but not read. And so she decided that was permission enough.

She pulled her car into reverse and backed out of the parking space, headed toward Sheridan and the childhood home of Cameron Wakely.

## CHAPTER THIRTY

By the time the patrol car carrying Michael Brisbane and Officer Lyons reached the Armory, it was dark. Michael had thought the place was eerie before, but now, in the pitch blackness, the darkened old shack looked like something out of a horror movie. Headlights illuminated the various pieces of junk scattered around the yard, casting strange-shaped shadows everywhere. Michael took out his phone as Lyons cut the engine, and turned on his flashlight.

As they stepped out of the car, the other patrol car arrived. Lyons said, "Geez, I didn't even know this place was out here. Talk about hidden."

"Yeah," he said as he arced his flashlight around the yard.

He pointed out the dents in the trucks.

"I want to get photographs of this," he said to them. The officers nodded, and one began to snap pictures. "Photograph everything we can't take with us right now as evidence. If we have to, we'll come back in the morning."

They followed him up the bowed steps, which creaked under their weight. The front door was closed tight, and at first, Brisbane assumed he might have to use force, but when he tried the knob, it opened easily.

He went in and felt along the wall for a light switch. He found one, and flipped it. Nothing. "No light. I don't think . . ." He noticed a lamp nearby and reached under the shade to turn it on. He turned the knob, and nothing happened, confirming his suspicion. "Damn. The guy doesn't have electricity."

"How's that possible?"

"I don't know. He's a Doomsday Prepper. Maybe he doesn't believe in it. I don't—" He stopped as his flashlight illuminated something else. "Wait. Got a match, anyone?"

Lyons said, "I don't. Bynam, you smoke. You got a —"

Someone provided the necessary book of matches. Brisbane lit it and brought it to an old hurricane lamp. A moment later, the room was bathed in a warm glow.

"Yikes," Lyons said, looking around, echoing Brisbane's thoughts exactly.

The place was packed with junk, just like the yard. Everything from old milk jugs to crates of magazines to car parts and containers filled with assorted things. There was just enough of an aisle to allow them to walk through, single-file.

"This is going to take us all night to search, Agent," Lyons said.

He dragged his hand down his face. "Yeah. I see that. But there's got to be something here." He motioned around the room. "Look under floorboards. Look for secret hatches. Things like that. We have reason to believe that he might have some secret rooms in this place."

There had to be something here. The way Gus had reacted when he mentioned those murdered girls? He'd wanted to high-tail it out of his place, as soon as possible.

The men fanned out in the house, conducting their search. Brisbane stayed in the living room, wondering where, among the piles of junk, he should start.

Then the beam of his flashlight spread out over an old player piano, covered with dozens of colored jars filled with buttons, needles, coins, mingling with many framed photographs. He hovered his light over a dusty photograph of a smiling blonde teen, slightly faded with age.

Actually, all of the photos contained that blonde. There were pictures of her as a young girl, as a gawky teen, and then a graduation photograph of her with a young man in a Nehru jacket, with a dark moustache and a full head of hair. Brisbane squinted to get a better look. Was that . . . Gus Mason? About a thousand years ago.

Slowly, the pieces of Gus's lonely past began to fall into place. He looked around, trying to find something that would show his suspicions to be untrue. He opened up a drawer of a nearby roll-top desk and found nothing but more buttons and old pencils.

He pulled his phone out and tapped in a message to Beeker. *Can you get me a profile on Gus Mason?*

Beeker replied a moment later: *Sending it to you, right now.*

A moment later, it appeared. There was a long rundown on the guy. He cursed himself as he read it, wondering why the hell he hadn't asked Beeker for this information, earlier. There were a few articles attached to the profile, including one with a headline: *COMMUNITY MOURNS MURDERED SHERIDAN GIRL.*

He scanned it, confirming that Juliet Mason, the daughter of Gus Mason, had been killed at the age of nineteen. In 1983, she hitched a ride home from her job at the local diner, and was found murdered, two days later, along the highway. According to the article, there were no suspects.

Michael had the feeling that the killer had never been found. That was why Gus Mason had been so eager to come to the station and help out. Not because he was hiding anything. No, he simply couldn't stand by when other young girls were in danger.

And that meant that this whole search was probably a big waste of time.

"Shit," he mumbled.

"What's up?" Lyons said, coming up behind him.

"Nothing. Keep up your search. I'm going out to make a call. I want to see if Wolf found anything."

He shoved open the screen door and stalked outside. The temperature had fallen considerably, and now his breath puffed out in a white cloud, in front of him. Pulling his blazer closed, as if it'd do anything to help against the bitter wind, he hurried to the police cruiser, pulled open the door, and grabbed his phone from the charger.

He was about to type in a text to Rylie when he saw he already had one from her. *I got a lead for a Cameron Wakely in Sheridan. It might turn out to be nothing, I'm going to check it out.*

He stared at it, question upon question building in his head. Cameron Wakely? Who the hell was that? What made her suspect him?

But the biggest thing in his mind was that after everything they talked about, she was going to go there. At night. Alone.

He quickly dialed her phone. It went right to voicemail.

Letting out a curse, he tried Beeker, who picked up instantly. "Hey, Bris."

"Where'd she go?"

"I don't know. Some Cameron person's house. She was mumbling something under her breath. I didn't quite understand it. But she tore out of here before I could stop her."

"And you didn't think to go with her?" His voice steadily grew louder and more urgent as he spoke.

He let out a long breath. "I'll tell you what I told her. You two may be my favorite agents, but you're not the only agents I—"

“Not the only agents you work for,” he parroted, completing his sentence. “I got it. But could she be in trouble? Who was this Cameron person she’s looking into?”

“I don’t know. To me, it seems like a pretty long shot. It’s from a file for an incident that happened fifteen years ago. A father was killed, a kid injured, from a road rage case on I-86. There’s been no record of the kid, though, for years. There’s a good chance he doesn’t even live there anymore,” he said.

A good chance. But that wasn’t good enough for Michael. “You should’ve gone with her.”

“Sorry, man. But don’t overreact. I bet you the guy’s long gone. I bet you she’ll be back here, any moment now.”

“Text me the address,” he snapped. “I’m going to go over there.”

He hung up the phone and sighed. Now, he’d have to tell Lyons he was commandeering his police car so that he could chase after his wayward partner. He typed in a text to her: *I’ll meet you there.*

She probably didn’t want him there, but he didn’t care. He should’ve insisted she come with him. He never should’ve left her there, alone. He should’ve known. That was just the way she was. The Lone Wolf.

And one day, she was going to get bitten.

# CHAPTER THIRTY ONE

Darkness had fallen by the time Rylie arrived at the address Beeker had jotted down for her. Number 1124 was at the very end of Big Sky Avenue, a street that was partly comprised of old, broken-down bungalows with weedy lawns and dark windows. Most of the real estate, there, though, was occupied by brand new, windowless warehouses behind chain-link fences and empty fields, filled with oil drums and bald tires. There was a brick automotive parts store on one corner, but it had an AVAILABLE sign in the window and looked as though it had been that way for ages.

She stopped her car at the address and looked up at the house. It was dark, and probably abandoned. Several of the other houses around it had boards over the windows. Maybe once, long ago, the place had been a nice, growing neighborhood, but somewhere along the line, corporate America had moved in and planted enormous warehouses there. Rylie looked at the old, rusting carcass of a banana-seated kid's bicycle, resting up against the front porch, wondering when it had last been ridden. It looked like ages ago.

*Okay, so this is a big bust,* she thought, slowly taking off her seatbelt and pushing open the door. As she did, she saw movement, down the street.

She stiffened. But when it came underneath the one working streetlight on the road, she realized it was just a stray dog, poking through the weeds for scraps.

*I sure hope Brisbane is having better luck than I am,* she thought, turning back toward the house.

She climbed up the short staircase to the front porch and pressed the button for the doorbell. The wind was whistling, so she couldn't be sure, but she didn't hear anything. Was the bell working? She knocked. Hard, then harder.

No one answered.

Unable to resist, she reached down and pulled at the doorknob. It was locked. She walked along the porch, her heels clicking on the wooden planks, and tried to peer in the nearest window. But the shade had been pulled tight. She went to the next and found the same.

*Yep. Big waste of time.*

She walked to the side exit of the porch and stepped onto a long driveway that ended at a single-bay garage. She walked along the gravel drive and to the garage door. It had no windows. She crouched, grabbed the handle, and tried to pull it. But it didn't give.

As she was straightening, something pricked at the back of her neck. She'd had that feeling before, a warning, that day in the RV. It was distinct, making her body quake involuntarily.

It felt like she was being watched.

She looked up, at the bungalow. All the windows were dark. She couldn't tell if it was the reflection of the bare tree branches, waving in the moonlight, but for a split second, she thought she saw movement.

She stood there for a moment, then stepped over the overgrown lawn toward the back door. There was a window there, but some heavy curtains had been pulled over it. When she tried the knob, predictably, it didn't open.

*Now, I'm really wasting my time.*

Rylie turned back for her car. As she neared the front of the house, she could've sworn she heard a door behind her creak open.

By then, though, she'd been more than a little creeped out. If someone was there, why wouldn't they answer the door? No, her imagination was just playing tricks on her. The place was empty.

She got into her car and started the engine. As she was pulling away, she saw two headlights.

Behind her.

That was odd. Just moments before, there'd been no one on the street at all.

She strained against the blinding light of the car's headlights to make out the features of the car. The headlights were at her level, so she could just make out the form of the truck.

A truck.

Sucking in a breath, she told herself it was fine. Whoever this person was had probably come from one of the other houses. Nothing to worry about.

She sped up a little, and the truck simply followed at a polite distance behind.

No problem.

*It's really nothing to worry about. I'll just turn here, practice my evasive driving techniques from Quantico, and leave him behind.*

She made a turn onto the next cross-street, which she hoped would be a roundabout way to get herself on the interstate. Sure enough, the truck went straight. She heaved a sigh of relief, but as she peered at its side in the rearview mirror, her stomach dropped.

It was an old-model, heavy-duty, contractor's truck, light gray in color, all tricked out with accessories. But the thing she noticed most of all? The dents in its side, and the black cage over its front grill.

Had he come from the old Wakelys' home? Where was he headed? Had he seen her?

Her first instinct was to stop, turn around, follow him.

But if he'd been following *her*, then who knew what he was capable of?

Still, if she went back to the station, they'd miss their chance. They could lose him forever. She'd never be able to sleep at night, knowing she'd seen their suspect and let him get away.

That feeling was just too strong. She quickly made a U-turn and pressed on the gas, tires squealing as she made a quick right turn, rushing to keep up with him.

This section of Sheridan wasn't very busy at this time of night, but it didn't matter. She didn't see any cars, anywhere. After traveling past the ramp for the interstate, she continued about a mile down the road, seeing no sign of the truck.

"This is so worthless," she said aloud, pulling into a gas station. She made a U-turn there and headed back toward the interstate.

As she was climbing the ramp, her phone, in the center console, lit up with a message. She merged onto the interstate and grabbed the phone to read. It was from Brisbane: *I'll meet you there.*

*Too late for that,* she thought.

She was just about to punch in a call to him when bright headlights filled the back of her truck. She looked up into her rearview mirror and blinked. High beams, scalding her eyes. The only time anyone used high beams when other cars were near was to be an asshole.

She braved another look, squinting to make out the cage around the front grill. Her heart-rate quickened.

It was him.

He was on her tail, just like he'd been on the tail of those other girls. On the same highway, no less.

She wrapped her sweaty hands around the steering wheel and tried to pick up her speed. The truck stayed right on her tail.

*Calm down,* she told herself, looking at the milepost. Two more miles, until her exit. *You're fine. You're not far away from the police station.*

She tried to keep the wheel steady as she reached over and dialed Brisbane's number. Then she held it to her ear, waiting for the sound of ringing.

Just then, a sharp impact sent her lurching forward. She dropped the phone and gripped the steering wheel tight, trying to correct and stay on the road.

She glanced up as the guy started to move to her left, into the fast lane. Any moment now, and he'd do what he'd done to all the other girls. Hit her back end and force her into an accident.

At first, she braced herself for impact, forcing herself into a defensive position. But then she realized she was just playing into his hands. No, she had something the other women did not. A truck. Not only that: she had FBI training and had dealt with psychopaths before.

Almost without thinking, she took her foot off the accelerator, going from ninety to about fifty in the space of a few seconds. The truck sailed past her. Then, ahead of her, its brake lights flashed.

He was waiting for her to catch up with him.

*No thanks,* she thought, slowing down even more. She looked in her rearview mirror. There were no other cars to be seen.

She needed to pull him over, somehow. Taking a deep breath, she rolled up next to him, intending to force him over, into the center median between the two roads. He went at a slow pace, as if that was exactly what he wanted.

When she got even with his window, she looked inside the window to see a smile.

That was all she saw. A bright-white smile that didn't fit the situation at all. It confused her.

*Why is he smiling?* She wondered, and it was in that split second that he swerved into her lane.

She wasn't expecting it. Rylie swerved to miss him, and wound up on a collision course with the guardrail. She spun the wheel to correct, too late. The side of her truck smashed against the rail, sending her truck ricocheting off its metal surface, and spinning wildly on the pavement.

Her head whirled, smashing the side window in a jolt of bone-crushing pain.

Blackness. Spinning lights. Squealing tires. The smell of gasoline and burnt rubber. Then she felt herself sliding sideways down an embankment. Stupidly, she punched on the brakes, but it was doing no good. She clenched the steering wheel, willing for it to stop, but it was out of her control, now. When the car stopped moving, she smelled smoke. Despite the pain in her neck and head, she felt a warm, comfortable heat.

*Danger.*

The word hovered at the front of her mind, but she could do nothing about it. She willed her eyes to open, her body to move, but it felt like her brain was independent of her body, spouting warnings that she had no ability to heed.

Finally, she cracked an eyelid open. Something bright. Headlights? No . . . too orange for that.

*Fire.*

Her car was on fire.

Movies always showed cars bursting into bright orange, exploding fireballs, but the reality of it was that few cars ignited that way. That was more for dramatic purposes, her instructors at the academy had said. Still, it was better not to be in a situation to test it.

But as she opened her eyes wider, she realized that was exactly where she was.

She tried to will her hands to move, to find her seatbelt, but her upper body was pinned by the steering wheel. She opened her mouth, tried to mouth the word, *Help*, but all she felt was warm drool—or was it blood?—falling over her bottom lip.

As she lay there, crumpled and twisted around the remains of her broken truck, for a moment, she wondered if this was the end. If she'd die here, like so many on this Highway Thru Hell. Then, beside her, the door creaked and peeled open. Cold air rushed in, a shock compared to the scalding heat at her legs.

*Someone's here to save me. Oh, thank God,* she thought for one hazy moment.

Then she looked up and saw the smile. The smile that had started all this. That had made her question what she'd been doing and run her off the road. It came flooding back. She'd been chasing after a killer, hoping to get him to veer to the side of the road.

And now, she was completely immobile, and he was standing over her.

*Smiling.* The skin of his face raw and mottled, as if someone had tried to melt it off.

It came to her in bits, almost like a nightmare she'd nearly forgotten. *Cameron Wakely. In an accident. Burned over 90% of his body. There wasn't enough healthy skin to perform skin grafts . . . numerous surgeries . . .*

He leaned in. "Can you take the heat?" he said, his voice eerily pleasant.

She reached for her gun, but he got there first, easily lifting it out of her reach. He grabbed her by the waist and pulled her out from under the wreckage with relative ease, and then her world was upended as he lifted her into his arms. For a moment, she thought, dumbly, *Maybe he'll save me?*

But those hopes died within her as he hefted her, unceremoniously, onto a hard surface. Pain screamed up her back as she heard the sound of ripping duct tape. He grabbed her wrists, binding them tight behind her back.

*Danger.*

But her body refused to do anything she told it to. She could do nothing but let it happen.

Then, he slammed the door to the tailgate, and casting her once again in utter darkness.

## CHAPTER THIRTY TWO

Every cell in Rylie's body told her to go to sleep. Drift off to dreamland, a place much happier and sweeter than this cold, hard reality she found herself a part of.

But she couldn't let herself do it.

She knew if she did, she would be dead. She had to keep calm. Cool. And above all, *awake*.

Despite the chill outside and on the metal bed of the truck, the confines of the compartment she'd been forced into was hot and suffocating. She kept thinking, *Maybe this is what Maren had to endure.*

She tried to stretch out her legs and realized that those were bound, too. The side of her body she was lying on was quickly going numb. She stretched her shoulders, trying to wiggle into a new position, but her head throbbed.

It was as she was moving that she thought she heard a noise. A human noise, coming from nearby. At first, she thought it had to be her imagination, but then it came again.

A quiet breath.

"Don't move too much," a voice suddenly whispered from down where Rylie's feet were. "I don't think there's enough oxygen in here for the two of us."

Someone else was here.

She blinked, wishing she could see the person who shared the small space with her. At first, she thought that maybe she was going crazy, envisioning Maren here in her hour of need.

Of course, now, she could feel the woman's body, and realized she wasn't just a figment of her imagination. Her forehead was pressed up against a part of the woman's clothing—she could feel her body's softness, then warmth underneath. But how was it that she seemed so calm? Maybe she had been here a while. Maybe she had already come to terms with the fact that she was going to die.

With that, it occurred to Rylie, just who was sharing this space with her.

She opened her mouth, and was surprised when actual sound came out, though raspy. “Ivy?”

A long pause. “Yes. Who are you?”

She didn’t answer. Right then, she felt ashamed to be an FBI agent. It was bad enough that she’d left her phone somewhere in her truck and allowed him to take her gun off her. Then, to allow herself to be captured by the man she was trying to apprehend?

But now wasn’t the time to beat herself up. It was time to think. If only she could force away the pain in her head long enough to string together a plan.

“Listen,” she whispered, the gears in her mind turning. “This man is a psycho.”

The girl let out a humorless, “No kidding. That smile . . . ”

“He isn’t going to let us go. The next time that door opens, he’s going to kill us. We have to do something. Are you bound?”

“Yeah. Legs and wrists.”

Rylie moved her face close against the girl’s body and felt the heaviness of denim. She was wearing jeans. She stretched her neck up and the top of her head grazed what felt like the ties of the girl’s sneakers. She pushed her nose up and felt the texture of the duct tape. As she moved her nose, bumping it lightly against the tape, she realized she could find the end where the duct tape had been applied around the girl’s ankles. She lifted her chin and nibbled slightly.

“I think I might be able to bite it and pull it open so I can get your legs loose.”

The girl let out a little sob. “Are you kidding me?”

“No. Keep your legs still.” Her teeth clasped the edge and pulled. It stayed tight. This wasn’t going to work. “Can you try to find mine?”

“No . . .,” A pause. Some movement. “Wait. Yes. Yours isn’t that tight. Hold on.”

As she tried to pry up the end of the duct tape with her teeth, she felt a slight tugging at her ankles. Her mouth and the denim became wet with saliva, but she kept trying to bite at it, lift it up with her tongue. After a few moments, she heard the sound of the tape, coming apart, down by her ankles. She could move her legs, slightly. “I think it’s working.”

“It is,” the girl said, her voice muffled. “Stay still.”

But suddenly, underneath them, the truck’s brakes squealed.

They were stopping.

Rylie felt the girl stiffen and stop her work. They both lay there, frozen, wondering what would happen next. Judging from the way the other girls had gone, she knew it wouldn't be anything good.

Then the truck's door opened and slammed closed, and there was the sound of footsteps crunching over gravel. He was coming closer.

Ivy let out a little whimper. "Oh, no."

The tailgate fell down, and the man with the scarred face and creepy leer stared back at them in the moonlight.

"Hello, girls," he said, pleasantly, dipping his head down to inspect each of them.

She purposely avoided looking at his face, knowing that creepy grin would shake her too much. "You need to let us go," Rylie said, keeping her voice even.

He held up a finger, and his grin widened. "No, I don't. The only question I have in mind is which one of you I should take care of, first? The nosy Fed who tracked me down, or the little hot-rod bitch Valerie?"

Valerie. The name went through Rylie's head like a lightning bolt. She remembered the article she'd read, back at the police station: *The suspected instigator, Valerie Hopkins, 22, was charged with manslaughter, but those charges were dropped late yesterday.*

He thought all of these girls *were* Valerie. That they were responsible for the death of his father.

Rylie swallowed. "She's not Valerie," she said cautiously. "Her name is Ivy."

Ignoring that statement, he reached over and pulled at her, yanking her towards the edge of the tailgate. Ivy let out another cry of anguish as he smoothed her hair. "You're Valerie," he said, almost sweetly. "You're the one who gave my father the finger, didn't you? You made him so angry. He wanted to run you off the road. And look what happened. Do you see what happened to me? Look at me!"

He shook her, forcing her to look into his eyes as she trembled and sobbed.

"Did you hear me!" Rylie shouted now, scooting closer so she could see him. "That's Ivy! Not Valerie. You have the wrong person."

He hefted her closer to him and wrapped his hands around her neck.

"Cameron Wakely!" she screamed. "Stop!"

But he wasn't listening. He turned Ivy so that she was facing Rylie and began to choke her. Still smiling, the excitement on his face as almost palpable, as if he was in pure heaven. His eyes seemed to roll back in his head and his sick smile grew. The girl's face went from pale to red in a matter of moments, and her bulging eyes fastened on Rylie, pleading for help.

It was as Rylie was trying to shuffle forward that she realized something.

Ivy had almost done it, biting at the duct tape. She hadn't thought much of that plan, hadn't expected it to work, but her legs were almost free.

It was then that Rylie knew what she had to do.

She rolled onto her backside and tried to flail her legs in a scissoring motion, pulling at the duct tape with every movement. The tape came free, sticking to her legs but allowing her to finally move. Slipping to the edge of the tailgate, getting Cameron Wakely in her sights, she struck, kicking at him as hard as she could.

It was enough. She hit him in the ribs and he buckled to the side, letting out a moan as he lost his grip on Ivy, who fell to the dirt, choking and gasping.

He growled and whirled to face her. But by then, she'd jumped to her feet. Wrists still bound behind her, she delivered a hard shoulder to his chest, making him stagger back.

The smile never left, but the eyes filled with rage.

"What do you think you're doing?" he hissed out through tightly clenched teeth, advancing on her. "I guess I should've killed you, first, huh?"

She backed up, gauging her next move. She could try to hit him again with a shoulder, but without the element of surprise, she doubted it would work a second time. She'd just decided on a kick when he lunged at her.

Her kick missed its mark and his hands wrapped around her shoulders, drawing him to her. She screamed and tried to move away, but dizzy, with her wrists bound, she couldn't manage to slip from his grasp. His hands tangled in her hair, pulling it.

He yanked her back flush against his body, and whispered in her ear, his breath hot and rancid. "You want it first? Well, you've got it."

Exhausted, mind hazy, hands uselessly tied behind her, she could do nothing but tremble as she felt his callused hands wrap around her throat.

"I'm going to enjoy this, Valerie," he whispered, as he began to squeeze.

Her vision was already fuzzy from the head injury, her body already weak, so he didn't have to exact much pressure before she felt it. The end was near.

She tried to drag in a breath, but her airway was blocked. Her lungs began to burn. The most pain she'd ever felt, like an elephant sitting on her chest. It nearly drove her mad, wishing she could claw at her chest, but her wrists tugged against the restraints at her back, useless. Her feet kicked at the dirt until the pain faded to a dull ache. A moment later, her limbs felt weightless and numb. For a moment, she thought she was floating.

She'd told herself not to close her eyes, but now, she couldn't help it.

She felt them begin to sag, heavy. Closing, closing, almost over.

Through the veil of her eyelashes, she saw a figure, in the distance, bathed in a white light. She was floating, as if upon a cloud.

It was her mother, smiling, beautiful, her dark hair curling around her face. She was reaching out a hand to her. Her lips didn't move, but her warm smile seemed to say, *Rylie. It's all right. Come here. We are waiting for you.*

But then her vision seemed to clear, and the white light faded. She saw the dark plain ahead, the chocolate mountains melting into the dark velvet blue sky. Her mother was gone, replaced by a tall man, wearing a suit.

He was standing, legs slightly apart, facing them. Holding a gun, pointing directly at her.

A gunshot went off, but it sounded as quiet as if it'd been fired into a pillow. She couldn't even be sure her ears worked properly anymore, or that anything of hers was in the place it was supposed to be.

All she knew was that the pressure on her throat seemed to ease. Instinctively, she sucked in the biggest breath of sweet air she'd ever taken.

Another gunshot. Softer, now.

And then she was on the ground, in the soft dirt. Falling there hadn't even hurt. She couldn't remember doing it. But she could breathe. That was something. A good thing. She was alive.

It was with that knowledge that she finally allowed her eyes to fully close.

# CHAPTER THIRTY THREE

An hour later, Rylie sat at the back of an ambulance with a bandage on her head, holding an ice pack to her temple. She was beaten up, her thinking still muddy, her head aching.

As she watched the EMTs wheel Ivy into the other ambulance, a car skidded to a stop on the side of the road. A young man jumped out, screaming, "Ivy!"

The he ran to her and embraced her.

Rylie smiled. Now, there was a happy ending if ever she'd seen one. Of course, Ivy would be haunted by the ordeal forever. But she was here. She'd made it through. And though she'd probably live the rest of her days with a lot more caution, she *had* those days, to fill with whatever she wanted to. She likely wouldn't take them for granted again.

Rylie's eyes shifted past the ambulance, out toward the overpass. There, she saw Michael Brisbane, standing with a couple of police officers. But he was smiling at the reunion, too.

When he saw Rylie looking, he jogged over to her. He gently punched her arm. "How you doin', slugger?"

She smiled. "How did you find me?"

"You called. I answered, but there was static on the other end. I knew something was wrong. I was already on the way to Wakely's house because I spoke to Beeker, and he gave me the address. As luck would have it, I passed his car on the highway. Just luck, I guess."

"Well . . . what can I say? Nice shooting, Tex." He shrugged humbly. "That *was* you, wasn't it? I was hallucinating a little toward the end there. Thought I was looking at Roy Rogers."

He clasped his hands together and extended the pointer fingers like a mock pistol, and blew the smoke from his fingertips. "I know. I was . . . tenth in my class at the Academy."

She gazed at him. "Maybe I didn't need to know that bit of information," she said with a shudder. How close had he come to shooting *her*? She didn't want to know. "Is Wakely dead?"

He nodded solemnly.

She sighed and shook her head. "That's so sad. His whole situation is sad. He did some very terrible things, but he was clearly a very sick man who'd been through hell. You think Ivy's going to be okay?"

"Eventually. Yeah. She just had a couple of bruises. The doctors'll fix her right up."

If only it was that easy. "Good."

"Your truck, on the other hand . . ."

She cringed. "Bad?"

"Totaled."

She shrugged. "It was leased by the FBI."

"I'm sure they'll send us another one so we can get back to the field office. They won't leave us stranded out here."

She lowered the ice pack and touched her bruise tenderly. "If only they could pull that kind of magic with this."

He chuckled. "You should listen to the EMTs and go to the hospital."

She waved him off. "What for? I'm fine. I just hate looking like I was in a fight, and lost."

"You kind of were. But you know what?" He sat beside her on the back bumper of the ambulance, crossed his arms over his chest, and leveled a gaze at her. "You always say that. And sometimes you're clearly not fine. And it's such a little thing. So maybe, if we're going to be partners and trust each other a little more, you should start by telling the truth about that."

She shrugged. She'd always been closed off, keeping her cards close to her chest, ever since the tragedy. How could he expect her to change the way she was?

But she had to admit, he was right. Maybe he didn't have to know everything about her, but in order to be a good partner, she could share some things. Maybe not all her deepest, darkest secrets. He'd already helped her out of enough tough squeezes to last a lifetime, and Beeker had spoken the truth—he was a good guy, an honest guy, impossible to dislike. So she figured that if there was anyone in this world she could trust besides Hal, Michael Brisbane was probably it.

So she took a deep breath, then let it out slowly, and nodded, conceding. "Okay, agreed."

"Yeah?" He raised an eyebrow at her. "So . . . how are you doing?"

She winced, and allowed herself to feel every ache, even the ones deep in her heart. "I've felt better."

"Yeah?"

"Truthfully, I feel like shit."

He grinned. "Now, that's what I like to hear."

She elbowed him in the arm and laughed. As painful as it was, there was a part of her, one she might've forgotten, a long time ago, that actually felt pretty good.

*

True to their word, the FBI provided Rylie with a new car before the following day was out. This one was a black sedan, a lot less exciting than her truck. The moment she started driving it, she felt like her backside was on the ground. She preferred to be up, positioned over the rest of traffic, so she could see what was going on. She took a picture of it and sent it to Brisbane, who was tying up some loose ends at the station. *Look at this awful thing.*

He responded with: *Looks like mine.* Then: *I never figured you for a diva.*

"I'm not a diva," she said aloud as she squeezed into the seat, feeling like a fish out of water. "I just want a truck."

Sighing, she drove toward the interstate. The plan was to get back to Rapid City by the evening. That left plenty of time to relax before heading out.

But when she reached I-14 and saw the sign that said CODY – 150 mi, she had a sudden inspiration.

Trying not to think about it too much, she took the long ramp to the highway and headed toward her hometown. On the long ride, she played music loud and thought about her father, during happier times, when he used to chase Maren and her around their property, pretending to be a coyote on the hunt. Or when he would make them pancakes with strawberry syrup for breakfast. Or when she lost a tooth by falling face first at the bottom of the school playground slide, and he carried her home and held her until she felt better.

Cody hadn't changed much since she was a little girl. There was the same barbecue place on the corner, the same car dealership, selling old hunks of junk. Her own house was out of the city proper. She didn't think she had the heart to go there, yet. But as she pulled into the apartment complex, she saw her father's red Ford Ranger, sitting in the lot. She pulled next to it, got out, and looked inside.

Her father was neat—probably from his military background. The black upholstery was spotless, and though it was an old truck, it looked ready for a showroom. The apartment complex was a two-story building with brown paneled walls and mustard-colored doors. Modern, probably, about thirty years ago. But now, it looked as if it'd definitely seen better days. The pain was peeling on most of the doors and there were grills, bicycles, sporting equipment, and unsightly lawn chairs on the balconies. She knew her father's place at once, because his balcony was the only one that was absolutely spotless.

She climbed the stairs and went to the door, and it was only when she knocked that she realized she had no idea what to say. She thought it would come easily—he was her dad, after all—but the moment he opened the door and looked at her, she felt woefully unprepared and tongue-tied.

Rick Wolf was just as handsome as ever, tall, with his dark hair and piercing blue eyes. There was more salt than pepper in his beard, now, and his belly filled out his trademark flannel shirt more fully. There were more trademark scars of his heavy drinking there, too—his eyes were bleary and his face, bloated, with broken blood vessels, dotting his nose. There was surprise on his face, but not the good kind. His eyes narrowed. "Rylie? Why are you here?"

"Uh—" She managed a laugh, and tried to be casual and lighthearted. "Thanks, Dad. That's some way to welcome me back."

"You think I should welcome you?"

"Well, yeah," she said, hardly able to believe he'd ask the question. "I am your daughter. And I came a long way. I thought maybe you'd be happy to see me?"

"Happy?" he spat. "Why? You high-tail it out of here without so much as a word to me, then don't check in or call for over a decade?" He let out a bitter laugh.

"You could've checked in with *me*, you know."

"Why? You made it pretty clear you wanted nothing to do with me, Rylie girl. You've been running from something, and I'm a part of that." He shook his head. "You know what? Sometimes I wanted to, too. But I guess you just proved to me what I suspected."

She took a step back, hugging herself. "What do you mean?"

"That it ain't possible to run away. Ever." He ran a scrutinizing eye over her, landing on the bandage on her temple, which had given way to an unsightly shiner. "Do you feel better? You sure as hell don't look any better."

She just stood there, regretting everything that had brought her to this point. At that moment, all she wanted to do was go back home. But what was home? It sure as hell wasn't here. It *wouldn't* be here, not with all those old wounds, gaping open.

And that's what she felt like she was doing, being here, now. She wasn't doing anything to heal them. No, she was just picking at the stitches, making things worse.

"I shouldn't have come here," she said, backing away.

She was about to turn and scurry back to her truck when he held out a hand.

"No. Wait. Rylie," he said, his eyes softening. "I didn't mean it. You just . .. surprised me. But you know. You always looked . . ."

*I'm the spitting image of my mother.* He'd said that to her, all the time. And as she grew older, and he looked at her less and less, she realized that every time he did, it hurt. It stabbed him straight in the heart. So she'd decided to do the only thing she could think of, to make it better for him. Leave.

But it hadn't worked. He seemed just as broken as he'd been, when she went off to college, that warm August day. She'd gotten into her beaten old car and drove west, expecting he'd be there to see her off. But he hadn't been.

"I'm sorry, Dad," she said softly. "I don't want anything from you. I just wanted to say hi. And that I was thinking of you."

She turned away and hurried back to her car. As she got behind the wheel, she checked her phone and saw she had a text from Brisbane: *Where the hell are you? Thought we were heading back this afternoon.*

That had been the plan. But she'd fouled it up with this bright idea of hers. And for what? So that they could fumble through the awkwardness of their broken relationship? Was she expecting anything different? It would always be this way, no matter how much time passed, no matter where they went to escape it . . . until they learned the truth.

And maybe that was what she had to do.

She'd had the resources at her disposal, now. She'd known, ever since she entered the FBI, that she could use them to look into her past. But something had held her back. Something . . . likely the fear that if she did know, it would be even more devastating than what she'd already experienced. Maybe it would render her completely immobile and lost.

Like him.

She didn't want to become like him.

But maybe, finding out the truth could help. And it was that she focused on as she started her car. She texted Michael, *I'm on my way,* and pointed her car east.

# CHAPTER THIRTY FOUR

Two days later, as Rylie was trying to creep into the old Rapid City SPCA/new Rapid City field office unnoticed, her phone dinged with a text. Loudly.

Nearby, on the floor, people started to look up.

*Damn, didn't I silence that?* she thought bitterly, inhaling sharply. It still smelled like dog around there. She sneaked behind a caged wall and grabbed the phone out of her pocket. She had a text from Cooper Rich, her friend at the Seattle office. He hadn't texted her at all since she left.

*Good work on that case. I probably don't have to tell you, but when Matthews found out, he punched a wall.*

She smiled. Bill Matthews, her old boss. What an incompetent jerk. He'd wanted to get rid of her for making him look bad, and he had. But when she'd left the Seattle office, she'd made it her personal mission to make sure that it wasn't the last Matthews heard of her.

*You just made my day,* she typed in, then pocketed her phone and crept toward the office cage she shared with her partner.

She *had* to creep, because she wasn't supposed to be there. Her new supervisor, Kit Brandon, who was quite a bit more level-headed than her old leadership in Seattle, had told her to take a few days off. Actually, Kit *demanded*, and when she did, people listened. The woman was tough.

It had only taken minutes for the news of the case to spread all over the FBI, and though she and Brisbane had been receiving all kinds of praise, Kit had been most impressed. She'd called Rylie personally to tell her not to rush back, and to take the week to recuperate from her injuries.

But Rylie hadn't been enthusiastic about it. She'd *just* done that, after the last case. And she couldn't help it. She was raring to get back to it. She'd been spending all morning, anxious, unable to think about anything else.

She made it to their office and cornered Michael Brisbane at his desk as he was taking a bite of a giant Hardee's hamburger. His lips curled up around the burger and his eyes widened slightly. He took the bite and chewed, wiping his mouth, trying to say something that was barely comprehensible, but she interpreted as, "Why are you here?"

"Hi," she said, peering out the door for any sign of Kit. She closed the door behind her and opened her mouth to speak, but by then he'd finished swallowing.

"Aren't you supposed to be taking those well-earned days off?"

"I already did that, last time, and it was dull," she said, sitting down across from him. "Why didn't she give you any time off . . . Mr. Sharp-Shooter?"

He pointed to her temple. "You're the one whose brains nearly got scrambled during that accident." He grinned. "Besides, she took *me* out to lunch."

"Really?" Rylie laughed. "Well, she sure knows the way to your heart. You must've gotten the steak."

"That's right." He pushed his burger away and studied her. "Okay. So . . . why are you here, again, when you could be Netflix binging to your heart's content? You still look like shit, you know."

She had to agree. Though the swelling had gone down some, her bruising had gone all sorts of interesting colors, yellow included, now. She placed her palms down on his desk. "Because I need your help."

He leaned forward, clearly interested. "All right. Pulling the partner card. I like it. You might wind up being a good sidekick, yet, Robin."

"Ha, ha. I think *you're* Robin."

"Oh, hell no. I'm definitely Batman."

She rolled her eyes. "Whatever."

"I hope this doesn't involve tracking down and shooting another serial killer?" he teased, his smile growing.

She pressed her lips together. Then she said, quietly, "It might."

His smile fell. "What do you mean?"

"Well," she said sheepishly, looking everywhere but at him. "I know you've been frustrated with me because I haven't been much of a talker. And I'm sorry, but that's kind of the way I've been brought up. But I do have a reason. Something that happened to me as a child."

"As a child . . .," he repeated, his eyes narrowing. "Something bad?"

She nodded. "Very bad."

"All right . . . "

He waited for her to say more, but she couldn't, at that moment. She was trying to build up the courage. Her heart was beating as fast as it had been when she was stuck in Cameron Wakely's trunk. She felt a little dizzy, like she might pass out, so she squeezed her eyes closed to try to regroup.

Finally, he said, "Wolf . . . what is this all about?"

She swallowed, and when she opened her eyes, she felt more relaxed. Though a lot of people had betrayed her trust in the past, the man before her wasn't one of them. Brisbane was a good man, and he could be trusted with this information. She was sure about that. But whether they could do anything about it . . . well, that was anyone's guess.

But they had to try. And she needed to start by coming clean.

"I need to tell you something," she said, taking a deep breath and letting it out slowly. "You know those cold case files we've been lugging around with all the murders that have happened in this area?"

He nodded slowly. "Yeah . . . and?"

"Well . . .," She managed a smile, because though it promised to be a long, hard journey, this time, she knew for certain that she was on the right path. "One of them is mine."

## NOW AVAILABLE FOR PRE-ORDER!

**SEE YOU**
**(A Rylie Wolf FBI Suspense Thriller —Book 3)**

**On a notorious stretch of highway rife with serial killers, victims are appearing across multiple state lines, seemingly no link between them. Rylie, pitted against territorial police departments, must tap her brilliant mind to crack the riddle, and save the next victim before it's too late.**

In SEE YOU (A Rylie Wolf FBI Suspense Thriller—Book Three), Rylie is assigned a new string of seemingly unrelated murders, but can make little headway with multiple state departments feuding over jurisdiction.

At the same time, secrets from her past that she'd rather keep buried are coming to light.

**Can Rylie keep herself sane long enough to save the next victim?**

**Or will the clock finally run out for good?**

A complex psychological crime thriller full of twists and turns and packed with heart-pounding suspense, the RYLIE WOLF mystery series will make you fall in love with a brilliant new female protagonist and keep you turning pages late into the night. It is a perfect addition for fans of Robert Dugoni, Rachel Caine, Melinda Leigh or Mary Burton.

Future titles in this series will be available soon!

**Molly Black**

Debut author Molly Black is author of the MAYA GRAY FBI suspense thriller series, comprising six books (and counting); the RYLIE WOLF FBI suspense thriller series, comprising three books (and counting); and the TAYLOR SAGE FBI suspense thriller series, comprising three books (and counting).

An avid reader and lifelong fan of the mystery and thriller genres, Molly loves to hear from you, so please feel free to visit www.mollyblackauthor.com to learn more and stay in touch.

## BOOKS BY MOLLY BLACK

**MAYA GRAY MYSTERY SERIES**

GIRL ONE: MURDER (Book #1)
GIRL TWO: TAKEN (Book #2)
GIRL THREE: TRAPPED (Book #3)
GIRL FOUR: LURED (Book #4)
GIRL FIVE: BOUND (Book #5)
GIRL SIX: FORSAKEN (Book #6)

**RYLIE WOLF FBI SUSPENSE THRILLER**

FOUND YOU (Book #1)
CAUGHT YOU (Book #2)
SEE YOU (Book #3)

**TAYLOR SAGE FBI SUSPENSE THRILLER**

DON'T LOOK (Book #1)
DON'T BREATHE (Book #2)
DON'T RUN (Book #3)

www.ingramcontent.com/pod-product-compliance
Lightning Source LLC
Chambersburg PA
CBHW030614310726
48979CB00003B/714

* 9 7 8 1 0 9 4 3 9 3 9 8 8 *